DOCTOR WHO
THE INVASION

DOCTOR WHO
THE INVASION

Based on the BBC television serial by Derrick Sherwin from a story outline by Kit Pedler by arrangement with the British Broadcasting Corporation

Ian Marter

W.H. ALLEN · LONDON
1985

The BBC producer of *The Invasion*
was Peter Bryant,
the director was Douglas Camfield.

Printed and bound in Great Britain by
Mackay's of Chatham Ltd, Kent
for the Publishers, W.H. Allen & Co, PLC
44 Hill Street, London W1X 8LB

ISBN 0 491 03324 9

Contents

Prologue

The Doctor sat hunched in his rickety chair, biting his nails anxiously and staring grimly around him in the crackling air as everything swam sickeningly back into focus. He uttered a whoop of relief as his two young friends reappeared, clinging on for dear life to the wobbling and sparking navigation console in the middle of the TARDIS control chamber. With a few spasmodic shudders the ancient machine finally shook itself together and settled, its harsh groans and staccato wheezes dying gradually away into eerie silence.

Jamie, a robust young Highlander clad in faded kilt and sporran, tattered sleeveless sheepskin waistcoat and sturdy boots, turned thankfully to Zoe and grinned shakily. 'We're all right, ma wee lassie. It worked!' he exclaimed, his voice cracking with nervous tension.

Zoe attempted a pale smile. She was a bright-eyed teenager with a large face, wide mouth and short black hair and she was wearing a tomboyish trouser-suit. She swallowed hard and glanced inquiringly at the thoughtful Doctor. 'Are we on our way at last?' she asked hopefully.

The Doctor still sat staring suspiciously at the motionless control column, his mouth drawn sharply down, his black eyebrows ruckled and his small hands knotted uncertainly together. 'I suppose I'd better have a look,' he murmured hesitantly. He looked rather like an old-fashioned fairground showman as he shuffled over to the console and fussed with the switches and indicators in his concertinad check trousers, worn boots and shabby knee-length coat, tucking the frayed cuffs of his grubby shirt out of the way. He licked a finger as if for luck and pressed a button, glancing apprehensively across at a video screen set into the chamber wall.

A large dark globe took shape against a breathtaking background of brilliant stars. The globe was pitted and scarred and ringed with a bright iridescent halo.

'The Moon!' cried Zoe in surprise.

Slowly the Doctor leaned forward, as though he suspected some kind of trick. 'The Solar Corona,' he whispered, adjusting the focus and throwing the lunar craters into sharp relief round the Moon's rim. 'We appear to be stranded on the dark side, I'm afraid.'

The Doctor's ominous words caused Zoe and Jamie to exchange uneasy glances in the tense silence. The disintegration of the TARDIS in their previous adventure had been a horrifying experience and now it seemed that the ramshackle police box had managed to reassemble itself only to end up marooned behind the Moon.

'What d'ye mean, Doctor... Stuck?' Jamie inquired nervously.

The Doctor was poking about among the racks of printed circuits inside the hexagonal column. 'I mean stuck,' he replied, sniffing with embarrassment as he pulled out a suspect panel and studied it guiltily.

Suddenly Zoe's eyes opened wide. 'What's that?' she cried, pointing to the screen. A small speck of light had appeared on the Moon's pockmarked surface. As they watched, it seemed to grow rapidly larger and brighter.

'Looks like a volcano or something,' Jamie murmured excitedly.

The Doctor ruffled his mop of thick black hair and blinked unhappily at the strange phenomenon. 'Not on the Moon, Jamie.'

All of a sudden Zoe grabbed the Doctor's threadbare sleeve. 'It's coming towards us!' she gasped.

There was a violent clatter as the delicate circuit panel slipped out of the Doctor's fingers. 'Don't fluster me, Zoe,' he chided her, picking it up carefully. 'The orientation circuits are jammed. It may take a while to fix.'

'But Doctor, we must move out of the way!' Zoe insisted. 'We've only got a few seconds!'

On the screen, the mysterious gleaming object seemed to

be almost upon them.

'It looks like a missile,' Jamie said, gaping in fascination. 'Someone's fired a missile at us!'

'Someone? From the Moon?' snorted the Doctor, peering intently at the faulty circuits. He flexed the small panel a few times, traced his finger round its intricate connections and then popped it back into its slot in the column.

'Please hurry up, Doctor,' pleaded Zoe, hypnotised like Jamie by the weird glinting craft growing in the centre of the screen.

'Oh, do be quiet,' snapped the Doctor, flicking a series of switches and glaring irritably at the inert instruments. Once again he removed the panel and this time held it up to examine its complex structure against the increasingly brilliant glow from the video screen. Suddenly he emitted a squawk of terror. Zoe just managed to catch the panel before it hit the floor a second time.

'What the dickens is *that*?' croaked the Doctor, gazing open-mouthed at the looming alien image. The next moment he snatched the circuit panel from Zoe. 'Don't just stand there gawping, child!' he shouted, struggling to insert it back into its slot. He kicked the control column a few times and rummaged his fingers feverishly among the switches.

Ashen-faced, Jamie clutched Zoe's shoulder convulsively. 'We're too late, lassie, we'll never make it...' he gulped.

The Doctor thumped the console and unleashed a tirade of insults against his juddering machine as it growled reluctantly back into operation. Then, like a crazed concert pianist he madly manipulated the switches and savagely kicked the column while staring defiantly up at the gigantic threat blotting out the Moon and the galaxies beyond.

Seconds later there was a colossal explosion. The TARDIS and its precious contents burst asunder into an infinity of separate fragments. In the place where it had been, a vast silver craft passed silently through space, as if it had never existed.

1

Home Sweet Home?

Only the sound of leisurely munching disturbed the sunlit air as the herd of Friesian cows cropped the lush grass, occasionally raising their heads to gaze placidly around as they chewed contentedly. Suddenly they paused and turned in unison towards the centre of their meadow where a small area of buttercups had become mysteriously flattened. A chorus of mooing erupted from the motionless herd, but a moment later it was silenced by a raucous trumpeting which quickly became a banshee wailing. A hazy blue outline topped by a fitfully flashing amber beacon gradually materialised on the flattened grass. Silently the cows watched as the chipped, lopsided police box settled and solidified and the beacon stopped flashing. Then, with one voice, the herd broke into a furious lowing in protest at the alien intruder.

Inside the TARDIS the three companions hauled themselves groggily to their feet.

'Well done, old girl,' giggled the Doctor nervously. 'Just in the nick of time.' He patted the console affectionately. 'Another nanosecond and we'd have been nullified!'

Zoe and Jamie looked daggers at the dapper Time Lord.

'Well, who'd fire a missile at us?' Zoe demanded after an awkward silence.

The Doctor smiled sheepishly and shrugged. 'Better find out where we are,' he suggested, fiddling with the scanner switches.

They froze as a strange moaning sound suddenly rose in the distance and then gradually died away.

Jamie frowned. 'Whatever's wrong wi' the TARDIS, Doctor? It seems to go wrong all the time now,' he protested.

The Doctor tried to focus the blurred images on the screen. 'It just needs a bit of an overhaul, Jamie, like any other machine,' he replied defensively.

Zoe glared at the scanner. 'Not much good if you haven't got any spare parts is it?' she retorted huffily.

All at once she jumped, stifling a scream. The video screen was almost filled by a vast cavernous mouth yawning at them.

'We are obviously not on the Moon anyway,' the Doctor chuckled, as the weird moaning sounded again and several more cows nosed curiously into the picture.

'Earth again,' Jamie groaned gloomily.

The Doctor nodded eagerly. 'It looks like England. If it's the twentieth century I could look up an old friend – Professor Travers – I'm sure he'd let me use his laboratory to knock up a few replacement components for the old girl . . .' The Doctor hesitated. 'Unless, of course, he's still a babe in arms!' he grinned, deftly removing two circuit panels from the control console and stuffing them in his pocket. 'Let's go and see,' he urged them, making for the door.

Zoe was still staring at the mooing herd on the screen. 'I wonder whether that thing we saw behind the Moon is in this time zone or not?' she murmured uneasily.

'You mean whoever took a pot at us could still be lurking aboot?' Jamie said quietly.

'Do come along, you two!' complained the Doctor, grabbing them each by the hand and dragging them after him.

As they emerged into the sunshine, the cows lumbered away still mooing with disapproval. The Doctor turned to lock the door, but the TARDIS was nowhere to be seen. Zoe and Jamie cast their eyes to the clear blue sky in despair.

The Doctor took the two panels out of his pocket, frowned at them and then tapped his nose knowingly. 'No danger of getting a parking ticket!' he mused with a grin. Then he set off towards a gate in the distant hedge with Zoe and Jamie trailing unenthusiastically in his wake.

They trudged along the narrow country lane while the Doctor hopped optimistically about, seeking a clue as to the century in which they had fortunately materialised. All at once a whining drone made them pause and listen. They scanned the empty skies.

'Helicopter?' Zoe suggested.

The Doctor shrugged. 'Post Industrial Revolution anyway, my dear,' he cried and breezily set off again.

The noise grew louder and suddenly a small covered truck swung recklessly round a bend and sped up behind them. The Doctor grabbed his friends and scampered into the hedge, urgently signalling with his cocked thumb. The truck braked fiercely and lurched to a halt some distance further on, its diesel racing impatiently.

Straightening his rumpled collar and sagging cravat, the Doctor scuttled round to the driver's door. 'Good day, sir, I wonder if you could help us...?' he began.

The young ginger-haired driver wearing sweat-stained teeshirt and oily jeans shot him a frightened glance. 'Are you trying to get out?' he shouted.

'Actually we wish to go in... to London,' smiled the Doctor.

'Get in quick.'

'Oh, that's most civil of you...' bowed the Doctor.

'Shut up and get in,' yelled the driver, revving the hot smoking engine.

Seconds later the bewildered trio were jammed into the noisy cab and being flung violently around as the truck roared through the twisting lanes. After a few kilometres the driver swung the truck abruptly onto a deeply-rutted cart track which bounced them sickeningly into a small shady wood.

Killing the engine, he jumped out. 'Get away from the truck!' he shouted, diving into the tangled undergrowth.

Totally mystified, the Doctor led his young companions in pursuit. They soon found the driver crouching in the bushes, wiping his freckled face with a rag.

'Is something wrong?' asked the Doctor gently, crouching beside him.

'Company Security are on my tail,' he gasped.

'What company?' Zoe demanded.

The driver gave her a sarcastic grin. 'There's only one Company isn't there, miss?'

The Doctor motioned the others to keep quiet. 'I'm sorry, but we're strangers here,' he explained.

The young man looked incredulous. 'Strangers? You mean you're not from the Community?' he muttered after a pause.

They all shook their heads.

'Then how the hell did you get into the compound?'

The Doctor smiled enigmatically. 'That's a long story, I'm afraid.'

Zoe glanced around uneasily. 'What's this compound? Are we prisoners here or something?'

The driver leaned closer. 'Those who haven't gone over to the Company are. Course, not officially. They just make it rather difficult if you don't have a pass,' he confided.

Jamie's clear blue eyes narrowed. 'What about yerself?'

The fugitive listened a moment and then grinned bleakly. 'I managed to get in all right. Getting out again's the problem now.'

The Doctor frowned suspiciously. 'This company you mentioned... What does it do exactly?' he inquired.

The young man stared at the strangers in disbelief. 'International Electromatix, of course. You must know about them. They've got a world monopoly in electronic equipment. They...'

The approaching howl of powerful motorcycle engines suddenly silenced him. Turning pale, he dragged the odd trio deeper into the thicket. They waited, scarcely breathing. Then all at once they glimpsed a flash of gleaming metal and bright black leather as two motorbikes zipped past the end of the cart track.

When all was quiet again, their rescuer continued. 'They've set up a whole Community of their own... research facilities, factories... housing complexes... inside a network of compounds. Most of the locals joined the Company.'

'What about the ones who didn't?' murmured Zoe.

'My people haven't been able to trace them.'

'Your people...?' the Doctor cut in sharply, eyes widening.

The driver bit his dry lips, regretting his careless remark. Cautiously he stood up. 'Should be safe now,' he told them. 'You three'd better keep out of sight in the back. I'll try and bluff our way out.'

A short drive through peacefully deserted countryside brought them to a high chainlink fence, slung between steel posts and topped with several strands of wicked-looking barbed wire, stretching into the distance in both directions. Electric gates barred the road. A heavily armed security guard strode out from the squat concrete blockhouse. He was dressed in a black uniform of thick glossy material with gauntlets, high boots and a ridged steel helmet incorporating a dark visor beneath which only his thin-lipped mouth was visible. On the front of his helmet was a silver insignia representing a zig-zag of lightning in the grip of a clenched glove.

The guard's faceless mask bulbously reflected the driver's pale smile as he showed his pass. The guard stared into the cab and then marched round to look in the back. He glanced at the stacks of papier-mâché trays and slammed the doors. The gates whirred open and the truck drove through.

It was barely out of sight before two similar guards riding huge motorcycles skidded to a stop just as the gates were closing. Jumping off they ran towards the blockhouse, leaving the massive engines throbbing in anticipation.

Huddled among the trays of eggs the three friends heaved a sigh of relief at their narrow escape, but their euphoria was short-lived. After a few minutes the truck shuddered to a halt again and the driver's frightened grey eyes peered through the shutter from the cab.

'They're right behind us. Get out here and you'll find the London road about five kilometres due east,' he shouted above the clattering diesel.

Muttering their gratitude the trio jumped out of the back and fought their way painfully through the tall prickly hedge just as the two motorbikes roared round a bend and coasted up behind the truck. Led by the Doctor, they set off for dear life across the fields in search of the main road.

'What's that?' Zoe gasped, as a dull thundering sound suddenly started up behind them.

'Don't even ask,' panted the Doctor without glancing round. 'I think it's a bull.'

One security guard searched the truck while the other glanced cursorily at the driver's pass.

'You come back with us,' he ordered.

'What for? The pass is okay,' protested the driver.

The other guard strode up shaking his head. 'Nothing,' he snapped.

'Turn round!' rapped the first guard.

The driver refused. 'You can't force me back into the compound.'

The next moment he flinched as a cold pistol barrel was shoved against his temple. 'We're not on International Electromatix property now,' he persisted, defiantly slipping the truck into gear. 'You've got no authority out here.'

The safety catch clicked off.

'You want me arrested, you get the police!' he shouted, revving the engine.

The next moment half the driver's head had been blown off all over the inside of the cab. The truck lurched forward and then toppled sideways into the ditch. A stack of papier-mâché trays crashed through the open back doors and hundreds of vivid yellow egg yolks started merging and congealing on the hot black tar.

Intermittent spots of rain were falling from the overcast London sky as the Doctor led Zoe and Jamie up the steps of a tall terraced house with flaking pillared porch in Bayswater. Tired and hungry, they stared gloomily at the nameplate above the bell-push.

'That's odd,' frowned the Doctor. 'It says "Professor Watkins".' He shrugged and pressed the button. 'Still, the telephone directory said number thirteen...'

'It would!' Zoe grumbled, scowling up at the tarnished chrome 13 on the door.

They waited. The Doctor rang again and peered through the frosted glass panes.

'Och, dinna tell me we've come all this way for nothing,' Jamie mumbled dejectedly.

Just then a distorted white shape appeared behind the glass and the door was flung open.

'I happen to be *trying* to work.' The tall girl turned on her heel and stalked off down the bare shabby hall, leaving them stranded on the doorstep.

The Doctor cleared his throat politely. 'I'm so sorry, miss . . . We're looking for Professor Travers . . .' He motioned the others to follow him and ventured after her.

They found the girl in a large high-ceilinged room which was virtually empty except for several powerful lamps on stands scattered about and an expensive camera mounted on a tripod. Huge blown-up photographs, mostly of the girl herself, were pinned haphazardly around the white walls.

'And now the beastly thing's jammed!' snapped the girl, fiddling angrily with the camera shutter. She was taller than Zoe, with long fair hair, wide mouth and high cheekbones. Her dazzling dress was cut well above the knee and her shapely legs were clad in stylish knee-length boots.

'Perhaps I can mend it for you?' the Doctor suggested, wincing at the colourful geometrical pattern on her dress.

'It was on automatic shutter.'

'I see,' smiled the Doctor. 'Taking pictures of yourself?'

'Until you interrupted me. Then it stuck.'

The Doctor examined the camera while Zoe glanced at the photographs admiringly and Jamie gaped open-mouthed at the flamboyant figure as she re-arranged her hair in a huge mirror propped against the ornate mantelpiece.

'By the way, if you've come to see my uncle he's not here,' the girl informed them abruptly. 'I presume you're another nut, a fellow boffin,' she said disapprovingly, glancing at the Doctor's dishevelled reflection.

'I'm seeking Professor Travers's help,' murmured the Doctor, poking thoughtfully at the camera's mechanism with his penknife.

'Travers has gone to the States for a year with his daughter,' shrugged the girl.

Jamie nudged Zoe irritably. 'Och, another wild-goose chase,' he muttered bitterly.

The girl glared at the wild-looking young Highlander and then went on. 'My uncle – Professor Watkins – wanted to do some secret work and Professor Travers said he could use the lab in the basement here.' The girl elbowed Jamie out of the way and adjusted one of the lamps. 'I moved in because I was kicked out of my studio last week.'

'A'm no surprised,' Jamie mumbled darkly to himself.

The Doctor tested the shutter a few times. 'What field of science does your uncle work in?' he asked.

The girl grimaced and shook her head. 'He messes about with computers all the time. Complete nutter.'

'How very fortunate,' smiled the Doctor, handing her the camera. 'Professor Watkins may be able to help us. Is he at home?'

The girl shook her head. 'Fixed it? Great. Thanks.'

'Where is your uncle?' demanded Zoe impatiently.

The girl rounded on her irritably. 'How should I know? I'm not his keeper.' Suddenly her expression changed and she peered at Zoe through the viewfinder. 'Hey... Dolly gear!' she exclaimed delightedly.

The Doctor ruffled his hair in confusion. 'Who's Dolly Gear?' he inquired.

'Want to pose for me?' the girl chattered on, pushing Zoe in front of the lamps. 'Now throw your arms up and bend at the knees... Head back a bit...'

Rather resentfully Zoe tried to do as she was bidden, while Jamie watched with a satirical grin.

'Well, miss . . .' the Doctor persevered.

'Isobel,' the girl replied, her motorised shutter whizzing off shots of Zoe in quick succession.

'Isobel. Do you know when your uncle will return?'

'Nope. He left about a week ago. Haven't seen him since . . .' Isobel replied vaguely, manoeuvering Zoe into a different pose as if she were a mannequin. 'He was raving on about some new process these people wanted him to develop.'

The Doctor was restlessly tapping the two faulty circuits in his coat pocket 'Can't we get in touch with him, my dear?' he pleaded. 'It is rather urgent.'

'I tried the other day. They said he couldn't take any phone calls.'

'Who did?'

'Oh . . . International something,' muttered Isobel, clicking away again, as Zoe began to enjoy her new role as model.

'International Electromatix?' Jamie suggested.

Isobel ignored him. 'The number's scribbled on the wall above the phone. By the stairs.'

The Doctor heaved an enormous sigh of relief, thankful to have got somewhere at last. With Jamie close on his heels, he hurried out.

Zoe made as if to follow them.

'Don't move,' cried Isobel, still snapping away. 'You're a natural. I don't often get the chance to photograph a real model. Too expensive.'

Flattered, Zoe lingered on. Then Isobel paused and led her over to a battered old wicker skip.

'Let's find you some different gear,' she laughed.

Jamie stared at the hieroglyphic maze of names and numbers scrawled on the wall behind the telephone while the Doctor dialled.

'Suppose this is the same organisation the truck driver was telling us about,' he whispered. 'Perhaps the Professor's been . . .'

The Doctor nodded grimly. Then he suddenly flinched

as a harsh metallic female voice rasped in the earpiece.
'International Electromatix. State your business.'
'I wish to speak to Professor Watkins please,' requested the Doctor.
There was a brief pause.
'Party not available,' grated the voice.
'It is rather important,' continued the Doctor courteously. 'Perhaps I could leave a...'
'Party not available . . . Party not available...'
'Oh, fiddlesticks!' hissed the Doctor, slamming down the receiver. 'It's the curse of the Technological Age, Jamie. A robot answering machine.'
'I don't think you'll get any joy!' Isobel yelled from the other room.
Jamie sent a murderous look down the hall. 'What now, Doctor?' he asked dejectedly.
The Doctor rubbed his hands together expectantly. 'Nothing for it, Jamie. We'll have to pay International Electromatix a little visit.'
Returning to the makeshift studio, they found Zoe decked out in long curving eyelashes and a fluffy feather boa posing extravagantly in the glaring lights.
Jamie burst out laughing. 'Och, lassie, ye look like a wee chicken wi' all those feathers,' he roared.
Zoe took no notice. 'Any luck, Doctor?' she asked hopefully.
The Doctor shook his head. 'We shall have to go there in person I'm afraid, my dear.'
Zoe wrinkled her nose uninterestedly. 'I think I'll stay here,' she said, twirling the boa seductively in the Doctor's face. 'This is jolly good fun.'
The Doctor nodded in reluctant agreement and asked Isobel if she knew the address of International Electromatix.
'Oh, that's scribbled up on the wall somewhere too,' she giggled.
'Och, don't ye ever write anything down on paper?' Jamie exclaimed as the Doctor shuffled out.
'I'd only lose it if I did. The wall's safer,' Isobel explained. 'Can't lose a wall, can you!'

The two girls howled in mutual appreciation of the joke. Glowering humourlessly, Jamie trudged out after the Doctor.

The headquarters of International Electromatix turned out to be a tall slim tower of steel and glass surrounded by lower buildings, all faced with identical rows of reflective coppertint windows, situated in the City. Jamie and the Doctor paused to examine the huge bronze plaque above the entrance, with its symbolic zig-zag spark gripped in a giant fist, before marching resolutely through the automatic glass doors and into the deserted circular foyer.

Unknown to them, two men crouched on the flat roof of an anonymous office block opposite were observing them intently - one through powerful binoculars, the other through the viewfinder of a polaroid camera. They wore drab suits with narrow dark ties and both had short military haircuts. The larger man with the binoculars spoke tersely into a compact walkie-talkie.

'They're just going inside now . . . Tracey's getting them on film.'

The smaller man ripped the film out of the camera and hugged it under his arm to speed up the developing process.

The big man listened to his radio. 'Roger, sir. Benton out,' he said, switching off. Ducking below the parapet he crawled across to Tracey and examined the photograph. 'HQ want those two Top Priority,' he said. 'We pick them up as soon as they come out.'

Tracey uttered a curt laugh. '*If* they come out,' he grunted.

The Doctor glanced contemptuously at the plastic chairs arranged facing a semicircle of small computer terminals in the middle of the glass foyer. 'I suppose this is Reception,' he muttered distastefully, sitting in front of a terminal which had lit up expectantly as they entered.

'International Electromatix. State your business,'

rapped the machine.

'I wish to see Professor Watkins,' stated the Doctor.

'One moment...'

Behind a perspex screen above the terminals, tape spools jerked spasmodically back and forth.

'Party not available. Good day,' the machine announced at last.

The Doctor squirmed with suppressed indignation. 'Then I wish to see someone in authority,' he retorted.

'Key in identity. Request will be considered and appointment arranged.'

'That's no good,' insisted the Doctor, 'I wish to see someone now.'

'All personnel engaged.'

The Doctor's normally sallow features flushed with outrage. 'I insist,' he shouted. 'This is an emergency.'

'Inform exact nature of emergency,' instructed the mechanical receptionist, its spools spinning busily.

'It is a personal matter.'

There was a brief pause. 'Personal matters merit no emergency status,' the grating voice announced. 'Key in identity and...'

The Doctor's nimble fingers played a frenzied sequence of random keys on the keyboard. 'There. Work that out!' he snapped, leaping out of the chair. He strode over to the gleaming chromium-plated doors leading into the building itself and Jamie scampered nervously after him.

High above them in the penthouse suite of offices at the top of the tower, two men stood in a spacious clinical room watching the two intruders on a bank of circular closed-circuit video monitors. The combination of swept-back silver hair and thick black eyebrows gave the older man a disturbing appearance. His right eye was permanently half-closed, but his left gazed wide open with chilling pale blue iris and huge black pupil. His clothes were coldly elegant: a plain suit with collarless jacket, round-necked shirt and gleaming black shoes with chrome buckles. Head tilted slightly back, he watched the multiple images of the Doctor and Jamie as if they were specimens under a microscope.

'Do you recognise them, Packer?' he murmured in a leisurely cultured voice.

Packer, dressed in black security personnel outfit minus the helmet and visor, shook his head. 'No, Mr Vaughn.' His small black eyes gleamed with sadistic alertness, but his pale waxy face tapered to a weak receding jaw. His voice was thin and devious.

Vaughn sat down in a large padded swivel chair facing the vast semicircular chrome desk. Behind him the grey panorama of London stretched beyond the wide curving window through half-open vertical louvres. Reaching forward, he selected new pictures as Jamie and the Doctor walked down a long starkly-lit corridor, peering suspiciously around them. 'Most intriguing,' Vaughn murmured calmly, reclining his chair and staring impassively at the bank of monitors on the wall opposite. 'Deal with them, Packer.'

The Doctor was cautiously leading the way along the silent deserted corridor when, all at once, a glass wall slid across their path. Before they could even turn round a second panel glided across behind them, trapping them like fish in an aquarium. A sinister hissing issued from narrow vents near the ceiling and within a few seconds the Doctor and Jamie were overcome by a soporific gas. They sank to the floor, their fingers squeaking eerily against the glass barrier.

A few minutes later, Packer arrived accompanied by two armed subordinates. He inserted a special key into the wall and the glass shutters silently withdrew. With cold detachment Packer turned Jamie's motionless body over with his steel toecapped boot. Suddenly Jamie grabbed Packer's foot and twisted it viciously sideways. Yelping with pain and shock, Packer pitched spreadeagled on the floor. But before the dazed young Scot could follow up his attack, the two guards each grabbed an ear and yanked Jamie to his knees.

Packer struggled to his feet and gazed down at Jamie, beads of sweat breaking out all over his waxy white face. 'Wait!' he whined, balancing himself to kick his assailant in the face. 'This is going to be a pleasure...'

At that moment, Vaughn's velvet tones filled the corridor from concealed speakers. 'Packer, where are your manners? Escort our visitors to my office immediately.'

Packer froze, like a child caught stealing sweets. 'But I haven't interrogated them yet,' he pleaded, as the Doctor stirred and sat up groggily.

'At once, Packer,' Vaughn purred insistently.

Jamie helped the Doctor up, staring at Packer with defiant contempt as he dutifully motioned to the guards to take them up to his master.

2
Old Friends

Vaughn rose to greet the Doctor and Jamie as they were shown into his penthouse office. 'Please be seated, gentlemen,' he beamed courteously. 'Thank you, Packer,' he added coldly. His deputy lingered on the threshold until a dismissive gesture finally sent him resentfully outside.

The Doctor's keen eye quickly took in the artificial potted plants, the self-adjusting suspended light fittings and the comprehensive array of facilities ranged at Vaughn's fingertips. 'I knew there must be a human being in here somewhere,' he grinned, sitting down.

Vaughn bowed. 'I apologise for my staff's over-zealous behaviour but your arrival was a trifle unconventional.'

Jamie's hackles rose. 'Maybe, but there was no need to . . .'

The Doctor interrupted tactfully. 'I think perhaps we are the ones who should apologise, Mister . . .'

'Vaughn . . . Tobias Vaughn . . . Director of International Electromatix. I must say your business with Professor Watkins must be very urgent to force you to such extremes.'

Jamie sat up in astonishment. 'Hey, how did ye ken we were wanting the Professor?'

Vaughn gestured with well manicured hands towards his enormous desk. 'My computer reports everything directly to me,' he smiled.

'Everything?' the Doctor echoed innocently.

Vaughn nodded. 'But I regret that your visit has been wasted. Professor Watkins is engaged on a new project and he refuses to see anyone,' he said sadly.

The Doctor looked crestfallen.

'Perhaps I can help?' Vaughn suggested brightly.

Jamie nudged his silent friend. 'Och, it's only a couple of dud circuits, Doctor, surely a place like this could...' He trailed into silence as the Doctor glanced at him warningly.

Vaughn leaned forward eagerly. 'Circuits? Electronics?' he purred. 'My technicians are the best in the world. I am sure they could assist you, gentlemen.'

The Doctor shook his head. 'Thank you, Mr Vaughn, but the circuits are... are most complex.'

Vaughn gestured expansively. 'Complexity is our speciality,' he insisted, holding out his hands. 'At least let us try.'

The Doctor hesitated, glancing reproachfully at Jamie. Eventually he reluctantly handed over the two small panels he had removed from the TARDIS earlier. Vaughn seized them eagerly and examined them, his left eye narrowing to match the right. The Doctor noted the momentary shadow of astonishment that passed over his face.

But Vaughn swiftly recovered his composure. 'As you say, a trifle complex. But I am convinced we can help. I'll have them sent to our Diagnostic Unit at once,' he proposed generously.

The Doctor smiled weakly. 'You're extremely kind,' he muttered.

'Not at all. Any friend of Professor Watkins...' Vaughn paused, as though he were disturbed by the two silicon panels in front of him. Quickly he opened a drawer, took out a tiny miniaturised radio and offered it to Jamie. 'Do you have one of these, young man?' he asked.

Jamie looked blank. 'Och no, sir. What is it?'

Vaughn looked surprised. 'Disposable transistor radios. A market leader. Surely you've seen them? We've sold ten million in the UK alone. Modest compensation for Packer's excesses, I trust?'

'Most generous,' said the Doctor, prompting Jamie to accept.

Jamie took the radio and fiddled with it. Suddenly a raucous pop tune blared forth. 'So that's how it goes!' he grinned.

Wincing at the din, the Doctor leaned across and switched it off. 'And that's how it stops, Jamie,' he advised firmly.

Vaughn rose regretfully. 'If you'll excuse me I have an urgent meeting,' he declared. 'Mr Packer will show you out.'

The Doctor jabbed his elbow in Jamie's ribs and they stood up. 'Thank you so much, Mr Vaughn,' he burbled.

'Telephone in a day or two. We should have some news then,' Vaughn proposed as they shook hands cordially at the door. 'And may I ask whom I have had the pleasure . . .?'

'Not Whom . . . Who . . .' the Doctor quipped slyly.

Packer took them down in the express lift and showed them out through a side entrance off a quiet cul de sac. 'Next time read the instructions at Reception,' he snarled.

'Och, so ye can read, can ye?' Jamie exclaimed in mock surprise. 'And what other tricks can ye do?'

The Doctor firmly steered his rash young friend into the narrow street as Packer slammed the steel emergency door behind them.

'Friendly sort of chap, Mr Vaughn,' Jamie remarked, flourishing the miniature radio.

'Not what he seems,' the Doctor snapped unhappily. 'The normal human blinks naturally about once every fifteen seconds. Vaughn averaged less than one a minute.'

'Aye, and he's got horns and a forked tail too.'

'No, I'm serious, Jamie,' the Doctor warned as they walked towards the main street. 'Vaughn didn't even ask me what was wrong with those circuits or what they do. Beneath all that charm there's something . . . something not quite human.'

The next moment a large Jaguar saloon raced down the side street behind them and skidded up onto the pavement, trapping them against the wall of the IE Building. While

Tracey remained at the wheel gunning the engine, Benton and another man leaped out and manhandled them into the back before they could even protest. Then Tracey accelerated away with spinning wheels and smoking tyres. Jammed between the two bulky figures, the shocked and bewildered captives exchanged frightened glances.

Eventually the Doctor turned to Benton. 'And I suppose this is Mr Vaughn's courtesy car service?' he commented, with an acid smile.

As soon as his unexpected visitors had departed, Vaughn picked up the two silicon panels the Doctor had left on his desk and studied them carefully, a deep furrow forming between his eyebrows as he tried to unravel the curious structure of the circuitry. Eventually he looked up at the blank wall facing the panoramic window and a strange smile spread gradually across his lopsided features. He put down the panels and took an elaborate fountain pen from his breast pocket. Slowly he rose to his feet. He twisted the gold-plated cap of the pen and with a series of soft clicks and a subdued whirring sound the blank wall parted and slid aside.

Vaughn waited, gazing into the darkness beyond. Soon an oscillating hum began to rise and a fluorescent light started to pulsate in sequence with it. The air started to crackle with a dry electric charge as a fantastic structure appeared in the dark alcove. Standing about two metres high, it resembled a gigantic radio valve. Bristling electrodes sprouted from a revolving central crystal suspended within a delicate cage of sparking, fizzing filaments. Cathode tubes were arranged like a belt of glass ammunition around the base of the cage and the whole sparkling mechanism was supported in a lattice of shimmering wires and tubes. The planes of the crystal flickered with millions of tiny points of intense blue light and the apparatus possessed a sinister beauty as it hovered in the darkness.

Vaughn touched some buttons on his desk and the bank of nine circular screens flashed into life showing video replays of the Doctor and Jamie at their recent gate-crashing exploits. Immediately the machine in the alcove began to whirr and spark with increased excitement. Vaughn watched and waited, smiling expectantly.

Meanwhile, back at Professor Travers's house Zoe was still striking exotic poses with strange hats and the feather boa while Isobel shot roll after roll of 35mm film. At long last Isobel announced a tea break and produced coffee and a mountain of sandwiches.

Zoe collapsed gratefully onto a large psychedelic beanbag. 'Never imagined keeping still could be so exhausting,' she laughed, biting into a doorstep of crusty bread and mashed sardine.

'It's been a real treat for me,' Isobel complimented her. 'I get sick of photographing myself, but I can't afford proper models yet.'

'But you're very good,' Zoe said with her mouth full, gesturing at the large portraits around the walls.

'Oh, I didn't take those,' Isobel admitted with a wry grin. 'I have to model to earn the loot to pay for all this junk. I hope you'll be around for a while, Zoe,' she added, offering her another sandwich.

Zoe shook her head sadly. 'I expect we'll be off again as soon as the Doctor gets the circuits repaired.'

'Yes. Why are they so important?' Isobel asked, puzzled.

Zoe did her best to explain about the TARDIS.

'Sounds just like one of Uncle's lash-ups,' Isobel giggled dismissively. 'Daft as a brush.'

Zoe suddenly looked very concerned.

'What's up? Don't you like sardines?' Isobel asked brightly.

Zoe nodded and attempted a smile. 'It's just that the Doctor and Jamie have been gone ages,' she murmured. 'I've got the feeling something's happened to them.'

Isobel shrugged. 'Uncle's probably pressganged them into helping with his latest brainwave.'

Zoe stood up decisively. 'Sorry,' she mumbled, 'it's just that whenever there's any trouble around those two always jump right into it.'

Isobel drained her coffee and sprang up. 'Okay, Zoe. If you're really worried let's go and look for them.'

Zoe smiled appreciatively at her new friend. But inside she suddenly felt cold and hollow.

Several times during the hair-raising high speed journey through the North-Eastern suburbs and out into the country the Doctor had tried to extract some snippet of information from the three silent kidnappers, but all Benton would say was 'All in good time, sir, all in good time.' Puzzled by this politeness, Jamie kept mouthing queries at the Doctor, but he simply grimaced back at him to keep quiet. Occasionally a burst of rock music would issue from Jamie's transistor and then the Doctor would nudge him viciously in the ribs to turn it off.

Eventually the Jaguar bounced off the highway and sped through several kilometres of woodland until it suddenly emerged onto a vast airfield. The airfield was almost deserted except for a group of rundown Nissen huts, a few jeeps and helicopters, and a massive Hercules Transport plane in camouflage paint, with service trucks clustered under its huge wings. The ramp at the rear of its fuselage was open and to the Doctor's and Jamie's astonishment the Jaguar hurtled straight towards it, shot up the gentle slope and slithered to a stop centimetres from the inside bulkhead. Even before they had time to clamber out of the car the ramp had started to close behind them like a gigantic mouth.

An armed soldier with special shoulder flashes opened an oval door in the bulkhead and Jamie and the Doctor were ushered through into a long, dimly lit Operations Room. Along each side, rows of uniformed personnel sat at radar screens, computer terminals and communications units, totally absorbed in their various duties. Down the middle of the room, several officers sat at small desks on either side of an enormous Situation Map mounted on a perspex frame running down the centre. All personnel wore khaki berets and on their battledress pullovers a circular white badge indentifying them as UNIT 2 Personnel.

At the far end of the Operations Room, a tall officer with Brigadier's insignia rose from his sizeable command desk and strode to greet them. 'Nice to see you again, Doctor!' he boomed, his strong square-jawed face and neatly clipped moustache suggesting calm and confident authority.

The Doctor's eyes lit up with delighted relief. 'Colonel Lethbridge-Stewart!' he cried, scuttling forward to shake hands warmly. 'What a lovely surprise.'

Lethbridge-Stewart smiled modestly. 'Well, Brigadier actually, Doctor. I've gone up in the world since we last met.'

Jamie thumped the Brigadier heartily on the shoulder. 'Aye, the Yeti!' he exclaimed in recognition.

The Brigadier nodded politely. 'McCrimmon isn't it? Yes, we met in the Underground. Must be four years ago now, all that Yeti business.'

'Och, it seems like a couple of weeks.'

'Jamie, time is relative . . .' the Doctor reminded the lad.

'Are you still rushing around the Universe making nonsense of it in your machine . . . your TARDIS?' inquired the Brigadier heartily.

'Still travelling, Col . . . Brigadier,' smiled the Doctor modestly. 'But what's all this?' he demanded, spreading his arms. 'I'm beginning to feel like Jonah inside the whale.'

'Ought to explain,' Lethbridge-Stewart boomed breezily, motioning to his guests to sit down at his desk. He had a brief word with Benton and Tracey and they immediately departed. Then he ordered a Sergeant to bring some tea. 'Sorry about all the cloak and dagger routine,' he went on brightly, 'but sometimes my chaps are a bit melodramatic. Fact is that since all that Yeti caper I've been in charge of a new independent security force. Call ourselves UNIT or United Nations Intelligence Taskforce.'

'A world police force?' mused the Doctor.

The Brigadier laughed. 'Not quite, Doctor. We don't actually arrest people.'

'You arrested us right enough,' Jamie retorted indignantly.

'Not quite, McCrimmon. We've got International Electromatix under constant surveillance and we're keeping tabs on everyone going in and out. Your pictures were transmitted here and I recognised you.'

'Most efficient,' the Doctor congratulated him.

The Brigadier turned to him confidentially. 'Fact is, Doctor, you two were lucky. A lot of people have gone in there but they haven't come out again.'

The Doctor's eyes widened with fascination. He rubbed his nose attentively and sniffed suspiciously. 'Curiouser and curiouser,' he muttered.

Zoe and Isobel stood in the empty foyer of the International Electromatix Building frowning warily at the silent computer terminals.

'Golly, it's creepy,' Isobel murmured with a shiver. 'I suppose everyone's gone early as it's Friday and Monday's a Bank Holiday.'

Zoe sat down at a terminal that had suddenly lit up as she approached it.

'It's probably the same idiot machine that answers when you ring up,' Isobel warned her.

'International Electromatix. State your business.'

Zoe spoke loudly and clearly at the blank screen. 'Inquiry reference two persons seeking information regarding Professor Watkins.'

'One moment...' blurted the artificial voice.

The two girls waited impatiently while the tape spools spun behind the armoured screen.

'No information. Good day,' the robot eventually announced.

Zoe flushed with irritation. 'Now listen to me, you boneheaded fruit machine, I asked a simple question and I want a simple answer.'

The terminal repeated its terse message and fell silent.

Isobel shrugged. 'You see, Zoe, it's hopeless.'

Zoe's jaw set with determination. '*It* may be, but I'm

not,' she declared and started tapping away at the keyboard in front of her.

Isobel looked scared and baffled. 'What are you up to, Zoe?'

'Just setting it a little conundrum in Algol.'

'What's Algol?' Isobel whispered, goggling at the complicated mass of symbols appearing on the screen above Zoe's flying fingers.

'A sort of language for talking to computers, only this is a pidgin version,' Zoe giggled.

Isobel noticed the tape spools whizzing back and forth with increasingly frantic speed as a cacophony of furious buzzing noises erupted from the terminal itself. 'It does seem to be getting a bit agitated,' she murmured.

'You bet it is,' Zoe chuckled, typing madly away. 'This problem happens to be insoluble! Delete square . . . Print out Y to the minus X variable one . . . Integrate on inversine . . .'

An unpleasant and sinister odour like melting plastic began to fill the foyer.

'Continuous integration . . . There . . .' Zoe concluded triumphantly, sitting back with folded arms to observe the outcome of her attack. 'That should give it quite a headache!'

Dozens of floors above them, Tobias Vaughn stood by the dark alcove listening to a harsh semi-human voice issuing from the glowing apparatus within.

'The images of the two humans have been analysed,' it informed him. 'They are known to be hostile. They must be destroyed.'

Startled, Vaughn glanced across at the figures of the Doctor and Jamie frozen on the video screens. 'Known to be hostile? But how can that be?' he whispered hoarsely.

'They are recognised from Planet Sigma Gamma 14.'

'Recognised from Planet . . .' Vaughn tailed into dumb astonishment.

The weird machine buzzed impatiently. 'They must be eliminated,' it screeched.

Vaughn pulled himself together and smiled cravenly at the eerily sparking structure. 'I shall deal with them,' he promised soothingly.

The machine seemed to glare at him for several seconds. 'Our plans approach completion,' it grated menacingly. 'Nothing must be permitted to obstruct them.'

'Nothing will,' Vaughn purred.

At that moment a buzzer sounded on the desk. Vaughn quickly twisted the top of the fountain pen in his elegant fingers and the wall quietly glided back into place across the alcove. Mopping his glistening brow with a silk handkerchief, Vaughn sank into his chair and composed himself.

'Enter,' he called calmly.

The door slid open to admit a tall, seedy individual dressed in a stained white laboratory coat. His greasy black hair was flecked with dandruff and he constantly chewed the ends of a bedraggled moustache.

Vaughn gazed at him with profound distaste. 'What do you make of these, Gregory?' he snapped, pushing the Doctor's circuit panels across the desk at him.

Gregory turned them over and over with his thin grimy fingers, peering through thick horn-rimmed glasses. Eventually he shook his large head and shrugged.

Vaughn's good eye narrowed. 'From my Chief Researcher I expect a more intelligent response than that,' he said acidly.

'I'm sorry Mr Vaughn but I've never seen anything like them before. Given time I'm sure I could...' he babbled wretchedly.

'Then take time, my dear fellow,' Vaughn interrupted kindly.

Gregory nodded, evidently relieved to be let off the hook.

'Take one hour,' Vaughn muttered threateningly with a contrastingly benign smile on his face.

Gregory stared back at his Director like a frightened prey. 'One hour. Yes, Mr Vaughn, thank you,' he croaked, turning and slinking out of the office.

As the door slid shut, a series of warning buzzers

sounded and the stills of Jamie and the Doctor vanished from the screens. Vaughn glanced up in alarm to see Zoe and Isobel at the reception console. Smoke was belching from one of the terminals and snapping tapes were tangling themselves into a froth of brown spaghetti.

'... Take more than a soldering-iron to sort that out...' Zoe was saying.

'Great,' cried Isobel admiringly. 'Wish I had my camera with me.'

Vaughn's face relaxed into a half-smile of ironic amusement. He flicked a switch and leaned towards a slim microphone. 'Packer, saboteurs in Reception...' he reported with icy contempt. 'Or are you taking your Bank Holiday already?'

There was a mush of static and Packer's frantic voice squawked in reply. 'I'm on to them, sir... I'll bring them up to you.'

Vaughn reclined in his comfortable chair and shook with silent laughter as he watched the tell-tale screens.

Clutching steaming mugs of strong NAAFI tea, the Doctor and Jamie were studying a large selection of photographs on the Brigadier's desk.

'That one's Gordon McLeod, Lecturer in Physics at Cambridge,' the Brigadier noted, identifying one of the figures frozen in midstride on the steps of the International Electromatix Building. 'And this is Billy Routledge, chap I knew at Sandhurst. Landed himself a cushy little job at the Ministry of Defence.'

The Doctor peered at the blurred hurrying figure. 'All these people went into the IE Building and never came out again?' he exclaimed sceptically.

'No, Doctor. Most of them did emerge eventually,' Lethbridge-Stewart corrected him, 'but there was something jolly odd about them afterwards.'

'Odd?'

'Yes, Doctor. Take Billy for instance. He'd been extremely helpful with our investigations into Vaughn's activities, but once he'd actually been inside the building he started being difficult... obstructive.'

Suddenly Jamie seized a photo from the pile. 'Look, Doctor, this is the man who gave us a lift in his van this morning.'

The Brigadier looked disconcerted. 'You know this man?'

The Doctor nodded.

'His report is twenty-four hours overdue,' muttered the Brigadier anxiously. 'Whereabouts were you?'

The Doctor shrugged. 'Somewhere out in the country-side.'

'Some of Packer's gorillas were on his tail,' added Jamie.

'Good man, 013. One of our agents,' confided the Brigadier. 'I expect he's onto something.'

The Doctor blew on his tea. 'Tell me more about this International Electromatix set-up, Brigadier.'

'They control most of the worldwide computer production, Doctor. They made their breakthrough a few years ago with something called Monolithic Circuit design and stole a march on the entire industry.'

Jamie flourished his transistor radio. 'Vaughn gave me this.'

'That's just a commercial sideline, McCrimmon. They've made a fortune out of teenyboppers.'

The Doctor coughed and nudged Jamie to restrain his temper. 'What's your interest in Vaughn and Company?' he asked the Brigadier.

'Well, they got so big I decided to run a routine check. It threw up some odd things.'

'Like the disappearance of Professor Watkins,' remarked the Doctor, sipping the treacly tea and grimacing with watering eyes. 'I don't suppose you have the authority to search Vaughn's premises?'

'I'm afraid not, Doctor. The man's got too many friends in high places. My hands are tied.'

The Doctor stared at the varnish-like deposit round the rim of his mug. Then he turned resolutely to Jamie. 'Well, my boy, if we want to find Professor Watkins we'll have to do it on our own,' he concluded.

Jamie nodded eagerly and gulped his sugary tea with

relish.

Lethbridge-Stewart smiled apologetically. 'I am sorry, Doctor, but I can at least offer you a little back-up support.' He turned to his Sergeant. 'Walters, bring me a polyvox unit if there's one handy.'

As Walters went forward towards the cockpit section of the Hercules the Brigadier reassured his visitors as best he could. 'We're on constant alert here, Doctor. The polyvox will put you in direct contact with us at any time.'

'Jolly good,' grinned the Doctor, shutting his eyes and sipping bravely at his tea.

A few minutes later Walters returned with a compact object resembling a small pocket torch.

'Here you are,' boomed the Brigadier cheerfully, pressing a button to spring a short aerial out of the end of the device. 'It's on a fixed frequency. Range about a hundred kilometres. Just press the button and ask for me.'

'Splendid!' cried the Doctor appreciatively, draining his mug with a last heroic gulp. 'As long as it doesn't play rock and roll it will come in very handy,' he added glancing severely at Jamie who was already on his feet and raring to go.

Lethbridge-Stewart stood up briskly. 'Well, Doctor, if you're determined to conduct your own investigation I'd better organise a chopper to take you back to London. Some more tea before you go?'

The Docter leaped out of his chair as if he'd been stung. 'No, thank you,' he replied in a strangled voice, snatching up the polyvox unit. 'Perhaps some other time, Brigadier . . .'

Zoe and Isobel stood nervously between two armed security officers in front of Vaughn's desk, while Packer hovered shiftily in the background.

'You and your friend the Doctor have put me to considerable inconvenience today,' Vaughn purred. 'First he breaks into the building and now you ruin a rather expensive installation.'

'Only because it refused to answer our inquiry,' Isobel

retorted.

Vaughn smiled. 'You are naturally concerned about your uncle, Miss Watkins, but I can assure you that he is perfectly well, if a trifle uncooperative at the moment. Indeed, your visit is most opportune.'

'Why?' Zoe demanded warily.

'The Professor needs to be encouraged to continue his invaluable work for us,' explained Vaughn blandly.

Isobel shrugged. 'I can't persuade him to do anything.'

Vaughn leaned forward. 'No, but I can. Now!' he murmured icily.

The girls shivered slightly as they heard Packer sucking air through his crooked teeth in eager anticipation.

'Mr Packer will take care of you while you're here,' Vaughn told them, nodding to his Deputy. 'He enjoys showing visitors round our facilities.'

Packer grinned hideously. 'It will be a pleasure,' he promised, as the guards seized their captives by the arms and propelled them out of the office.

'Oh, Packer.'

Packer turned round to find his master gazing at him with amused concern. 'Yes, Mr Vaughn?'

'Don't work *too* hard, will you?'

Once again the Doctor and Jamie found themselves staring with sinking hearts at the number 13 on Professor Travers's front door, while the bell rang monotonously inside.

'Och, they must've gone out,' Jamie sighed despondently.

Delving into his pocket the Doctor unearthed a small penknife bristling with different sized blades and all manner of attachments. Selecting one, he deftly poked it around in the lock and a few seconds later the door clicked open. They went in, calling and whistling, but the house was silent.

In the studio they came across the remains of the sardine sandwiches. 'I don't know what they are but I'm ravenous!' cried the Doctor, biting greedily into two thick portions at once.

'Sardines!' Jamie cheered. 'Delicious, I'm fair starved.'

They finished the leftovers in silence. Then Jamie took out his transistor and a deafening rock number suddenly blared out, causing the Doctor to choke on his last mouthful. Snatching it away from Jamie, he was about to fling the offending device into the grate when he changed his mind, switched it off and opened the back instead.

'Och, dinna wreck ma wee gift,' Jamie pleaded indignantly.

Ignoring him, the Doctor took out a watchmaker's eyeglass and carefully scrutinised the inner surface of the plastic lid. 'Most ingenious . . .' he muttered after a while '. . . but I wonder what it's for?'

'What what's for?'

'There's a micromonolithic circuit etched into the back of this casing, Jamie.'

'Aye, and what's that when it's at home?'

'A hyper complex miniature array,' replied the Doctor, taking out the eyeglass and staring at Jamie with troubled eyes. 'But it has nothing whatever to do with simple radio technology.'

While the Doctor fiddled about inside the radio, muttering to himself and taking absent-minded swigs of cold coffee from Zoe's abandoned cup, Jamie wandered aimlessly around the room scowling at the zany blow-ups of Isobel adorning the walls. Suddenly he stopped in his tracks. 'Surely they'd leave us a wee note, Doctor,' he suggested.

'On the wall!' shouted the Doctor, jumping up and tossing him the pieces of the radio.

Jamie gaped at him in astonishment.

'You can't lose a wall can you!' the Doctor quipped, echoing Isobel's words as he hurried into the hall.

Jamie trailed after him, gloomily contemplating the remains of his radio.

'Here we are,' the Doctor confirmed, twisting himself almost horizontal to decipher a patch of barely legible scrawl beside the telephone. 'Oh my goodness me,' he whispered. 'Gone to IE office to look for you. Z and I.'

The Doctor bounded to the front door and wrenched it open. 'Come on, Jamie, we must get after them!'

Jamie frowned wearily. 'Och, it's miles, Doctor. Could we no get a lift this time?'

The Doctor shook his head vehemently. 'No, we most certainly could not, Jamie. We shall hail a taxi!' he insisted.

3

Cat and Mouse

Crouching beside the Doctor between two huge rubbish skips in the cul-de-sac alongside the International Electromatix Building, Jamie ground his teeth in frustration.

'I thought we were going in there to find the lassies,' he complained.

The Doctor shook his head determinedly. 'We'd never get past that stupid computer, Jamie. Besides, the girls might not be in there. We don't want to aggravate Vaughn unnecessarily.'

'Then what the divil are we going to do?'

The Doctor took out the polyvox unit given him by the Brigadier, deployed the aerial and pressed the call button. 'If the Brigadier's men are watching the building they'll know whether the girls are inside or not,' he explained.

Eventually the Brigadier's voice crackled through a haze of interference. 'Sorry about reception, Doctor, but we're airborne at the moment. Routine change of location for security cover.'

The Doctor asked whether Zoe and Isobel had been sighted.

'Affirmative, Doctor. We have a report of two teenage females, one dark and one fair, clad in strange attire. Went in about an hour ago.'

The Doctor grabbed Jamie's belt with his free hand to prevent the headstrong Highlander from dashing to the rescue there and then. He informed the Brigadier that they were going to try and enter the building from the rear.

'Take care, Doctor,' crackled Lethbridge-Stewart. 'You

may not be quite so lucky this time. Give me a shout if you hit any snags.'

'Yes. Thank you, Brigadier. Under and off...'

'Over and out,' came the crisp response.

Jamie contemplated the Doctor with less than whole-hearted confidence as he struggled to stow the aerial. 'Pity it doesn't play guid tunes like ma radio used to,' he scoffed.

They stared across at the vast expanse of coppery glass towering above them.

'And how are we going to get in this time?' Jamie demanded sceptically.

The Doctor grinned mischievously. 'By train, of course. But we must hurry, or we'll miss it...'

Far above the City streets, Vaughn reclined in his chair listening to Gregory's bewildered report on the Doctor's two circuit panels.

'They just make no sense,' whined the wretched technician helplessly. 'The connections seem completely illogical and the conductor material is no known alloy, though it resembles Helenium.'

Vaughn took the panels and studied them, smiling mysteriously. 'Fascinating. The Doctor intrigues me more and more,' he murmured languidly.

'I can do more tests, Mr Vaughn...' Gregory offered anxiously.

Vaughn waved him away. 'I think I know the solution to this little mystery,' he said quietly.

As soon as Gregory had gone, Vaughn took out his fountain pen and twisted the cap. As the wall parted, revealing the secret apparatus, Vaughn rose and wandered over to the alcove. 'I require more data concerning the individual known as the Doctor,' he announced in a cold precise voice.

The machine fizzed and flickered before croaking its reply. 'You have sufficient information. The Doctor is an enemy and must be destroyed.'

'You state that you recognise the Doctor from Planet Sigma Gamma 14. How is that possible?' Vaughn persisted calmly.

'Your inquiry is redundant,' rasped the disembodied voice.

Vaughn's pale eyes gleamed. 'That is for me to decide.'

'You will obey.'

Vaughn stood his ground unflinchingly. 'Negative. I control the operation here on Earth. Unless that is agreed our cooperation is at an end,' he declared in a voice like cut glass.

The crystal at the heart of the machine revolved rapidly, emitting myriad points of intense light. Eventually it stopped. 'It has been agreed,' it rasped.

Vaughn smiled bleakly. 'I felt sure that your masters would be reasonable,' he purred. 'Now, how did this Doctor reach Planet Sigma Gamma 14?'

'He possesses a device.'

Vaughn's body tensed expectantly. 'What kind of device?' he demanded with suppressed excitement.

The apparatus whirred and revolved. 'No further information available. The Doctor will be eliminated. The invasion must proceed,' it decreed harshly, needles of light shooting from the crystal.

Vaughn nodded decisively. 'Oh, it will. The Doctor will be taken care of. I shall attend to it personally...'

With a vicious twist of the pen top, Vaughn banished the thing to the darkness again behind the wall.

Totally mystified, Jamie had followed the Doctor through a maze of alleys and back streets and finally up onto a railway embankment which snaked between warehouses and office blocks. The Doctor had skipped nimbly along the sleepers and led Jamie off on a single track branch line which curved sharply round and finally brought them into a marshalling yard enclosed by high walls at the rear of the International Electromatix Building.

'This is a private branch line off the main line into Liverpool Street...' the Doctor explained, darting across the rusting rails towards a line of freight wagons bearing the familiar fist and lightning flash symbol of International Electromatix.

'But how did ye ken it was here?' Jamie panted.

'I consulted the Brigadier's excellent map,' smirked the Doctor, using the wagons as cover to approach the extensive warehouse buildings at the back of the tower. 'I memorised it to distract myself from the taste of his execrable tea.'

Following the line of wagons in the siding they soon reached a vast covered loading bay adjoining the warehouse. It was filled with stacks of cylindrical metal containers each about two and a half metres long by about a metre in diameter. Each one had a short blunt projection at both ends and a specially shaped base to facilitate vertical stacking.

Huddled against the coupling between two wagons, Jamie and the Doctor watched in amazement as a man with crew-cut hair wearing a blue boiler suit emerged from the warehouse carrying one of the containers as if it were a baby. He placed it carefully on one of the stacks and then returned to the warehouse.

'Extraordinary!' marvelled the Doctor.

'Probably empty,' Jamie whispered.

'Let's find out,' the Doctor suggested eagerly.

Leaving their hiding place, they ran over to the stack and attempted to lift the container. They failed even to budge it.

'Yon fellow must be a superman,' Jamie gasped.

The Doctor tried to raise the hinged lid, but it was securely fastened. 'I wonder what's inside?' he mused.

The sound of heavy footsteps sent them scurrying behind a neighbouring stack, where they watched the same man bring an identical container and add it to the pile.

Jamie's eyes were popping with astonishment. 'Let's find the lassies and get oot,' he urged. 'That chap gives me the heebie-jeebies.'

When the man had gone, they crept between the endless stacks of crates desperately seeking a likely route into the main building.

Unknown to them, robot cameras in the roof were tracking their every movement and at the top of the tower block Tobias Vaughn was observing their progress on his nine monitors, chuckling with urbane amusement.

All at once Packer's reedy voice whined out of the intercom on Vaughn's desk. 'Mr Vaughn, the Doctor and the boy are back again . . . Surveillance spotted them in the warehouse.'

Vaughn laughed sarcastically. 'I wondered how long it would take your experts to notice our intruders, Packer. They've been entertaining me for at least ten minutes.'

'I'll issue an alert, sir.'

Vaughn sighed despairingly. 'Packer, do try to aspire to a modicum of subtlety,' he pleaded, wincing fastidiously. 'We need a sprat to catch our mackerel. Take the young ladies down to the warehouse and pop them in their coffins.'

Smoothing back his sleek silver hair and adjusting the silk handkerchief in his breast pocket, Vaughn strode across to his private elevator and selected Ground Floor - Express. His keen mind considered the problem of the meddlesome Doctor and his mysterious circuits as he glided earthwards.

When the elevator stopped, Vaughn had made his decision.

'This place is like a maze,' Jamie complained as he and the Doctor threaded their way cautiously among the identical stacks, keeping their eyes skinned for any more boiler-suited Hercules.

Suddenly they froze as two piercing screams echoed around the vast warehouse.

'Zoe and Isobel!' Jamie hissed, pointing back towards the loading bay.

Turning, they ran on tip-toe in the direction of the marshalling yard. Crouching in the shadows between the stacks, they watched as Packer supervised two men loading two containers into the last wagon of the train. Jamie gasped as he caught a glimpse of a fluttering string of feathers trapped between the lid and the rim of one of the metal cases.

'Doctor... Zoe's in that crate!' he exclaimed, standing upright with fists clenched and pulse racing madly.

'Jamie, wait!' growled the Doctor, grabbing his arm.

But the impulsive boy shook himself free and sprinted towards the wagons yelling at the top of his voice 'What have ye done with Zoe...!'

The Doctor chewed the frayed edge of his cravat in anguish as he saw Packer whip round and snatch out a pistol as Jamie bore down on him. Springing into view, he scampered in pursuit, shouting to Jamie to stop behaving like an idiot.

Two steel-helmeted guards armed with sten guns suddenly appeared between the wagons and Jamie stumbled to a halt. Turning, he saw two more guards appear behind the Doctor. It was hopeless. The two friends stood side by side panting for breath as the four guards closed in on them, slipping their safety catches.

Packer's weak face lit up in cowardly triumph. 'Rats,' he hissed, strutting malevolently towards them. 'Rats in a trap.'

As the guards forced their captives back towards the warehouse, Packer exulted in his victory. 'Don't you understand - this is private property, a restricted area,' he whined.

'What have you done with Zoe and Isobel?' Jamie demanded savagely. 'We heard them screaming.'

'Silence!' Packer snapped.

'We saw the box with...'

Packer lashed Jamie brutally across the face with his leather glove. 'I told you to be quiet.'

The Doctor gasped with shock as Jamie staggered against him clutching his ear, with blood seeping from his nose.

Before Packer could repeat the vicious blow, Vaughn's measured tones rang out. 'Packer, you really must try to curb this violent streak in your nature, though I admit the situation is a trifle provoking.'

Flanked by two armed guards, the Director of International Electromatix strode towards them, wagging his finger at the Doctor. 'You really are beginning to try our patience,' he chided menacingly.

The Doctor cleared his throat with undisguised distaste. 'We came to look for two young friends of ours, Mr Vaughn.'

Vaughn nodded. 'Two young ladies.'

'You see,' Jamie exploded. 'He admits they're here.'

Vaughn shook his head regretfully. 'Correction. They *were* here. You appear to have been chasing one another's tails. They came here in search of you.'

'And where are they now?' the Doctor inquired calmly.

'They departed.'

'Aye. In one of your tin coffins!' Jamie shouted.

Vaughn glanced scornfully at the Doctor. 'Really . . .' he protested.

'We did hear someone scream,' the Doctor quietly pointed out.

'And Zoe's boa is sticking out of one of the boxes,' Jamie persisted, wiping the blood from his nose.

Vaughn threw back his head and roared with laughter. 'What a fertile imagination you have, young man,' he said tartly.

The Doctor placed a restraining hand on Jamie's shoulder. 'Mr Vaughn, it would set our minds at rest if you would permit us to examine the boxes in the last wagon . . . in case there has been an accident,' he ventured tactfully.

Vaughn spread his arms generously. 'But of course,' he agreed readily. He turned to Packer who was sulking at having the limelight stolen from him. 'No doubt the Doctor is referring to the empty crates in transit back to the factories,' he said, with a significant sideways glance of his hooded eyes.

'Yes, Mr Vaughn. The train's due out any minute.'

'Then we must waste no more time,' Vaughn smiled. 'After you, Doctor.'

As Jamie and the Doctor eagerly set off back towards the marshalling yard, Vaughn signalled secretly to Packer and then caught up with them.

Packer pulled back his left sleeve, exposing a miniaturised two-way radio no bigger than a wristwatch. Pressing a tiny button, he whispered urgently into it. 'Traffic? Top priority. Get the return transit rolling at once. Do you hear me? Right now.'

Just as the Doctor, Jamie and Vaughn reached the loading bay there was a sudden clanking of couplings and the freight wagons slowly began to pull out of the siding. Jamie started running after them but he was far too late. He gave up and stood staring at the rapidly accelerating train with a sinking heart.

'What a pity,' Vaughn said consolingly. 'I am sorry.'

The Doctor's brow was deeply furrowed with mounting anxiety, but he attempted a wry smile.

'However, all is not lost,' Vaughn went on brightly. 'I have to visit the factory complex myself this afternoon. Would you two gentlemen care to accompany me? We can meet the train there.'

Jamie glanced apprehensively at Packer and his security guards hovering at the entrance to the warehouse. The Doctor squeezed his arm reassuringly and turned to Vaughn. 'Most kind. We'd be delighted to come.'

'Splendid,' Vaughn purred and led the way into the main building.

Brigadier Alistair Gordon Lethbridge-Stewart was sitting at his desk in the Hercules Operations Room, straining to hear Benton's voice on the radiotelephone above the whine of the mighty turboprops as the massive plane came in to land on a disused RAF station.

'How long ago did they go into the railway yard?' he repeated.

'About an hour ago, sir. Tracey followed them to the ... Just a minute, sir ...'

The Brigadier pressed the handset firmly to his ear and waited impatiently. 'Benton, what the devil's going on?' he demanded in clipped urgent tones.

'The Doctor and the boy have just come out of the main entrance, sir. Vaughn's with them.'

'Vaughn!' echoed the Brigadier in surprise.

'And Packer, sir. They're getting into Vaughn's Rolls.'

The Brigadier stroked his neat moustache thoughtfully. 'Are they being harrassed, Benton?'

'Doesn't look like it, sir...'

The Brigadier was roughly jolted about as the Hercules touched down and coasted along the uneven concrete runway. 'Benton...' he shouted irritably.

'All looks quite friendly, sir. They're just being driven off now. Shall we follow, sir?'

'Negative, Benton. Continue surveillance at your location. Out.' Unlatching his seat belt, the Brigadier leaped to his feet. 'Sergeant Walters, alert aerial patrol Section Three,' he instructed. Then he turned to a tall, dark-haired young officer at the Situation Map. 'Captain Turner, as soon as we're on blocks get aboard a chopper and rendezvous with Section Three tracking agents,' he shouted above the engines as they revved at reverse pitch to slow the heavy plane. 'We'll play it by ear for a bit so keep your nose out of trouble.'

'Yes, sir,' snapped Turner with a crisp salute.

'Should the Doctor contact us for help I'll have him connected directly to you.'

Turner strode away towards the huge cargo bay at the rear, briskly snapping instructions right and left.

The Brigadier studied the brightly coloured Situation Map for a long time, occasionally breaking off to receive a report or to issue a string of orders to the widely spread and versatile forces under his overall command.

At last Captain Turner came through, shouting above the din of the helicopter engine on the radiotelephone. 'They've just gone through the IE Compound gates, sir. They seem to be heading for the Factory Complex.'

The Brigadier's calm exterior betrayed a brief tremor of excitement. 'Circle the area but keep out of sight, Jimmy,' he advised. 'If you're spotted it might make things worse for our two friends. We can't do anything until we get a request for assistance.'

He signed off and took a sip of cold tea from his chipped mug. 'After all, this is all rather unofficial...' he murmured wryly to himself.

The Doctor remained silent during the short high-speed drive out of London, his eyes fixed steadfastly on the disturbing International Electromatix symbol on the pennant flying from the front wing of the enormous white Rolls Royce.

'The train with the empty containers will not arrive for some time,' Vaughn informed him as they drew up in front of what appeared to be a smaller version of the Company's City headquarters. 'Meanwhile, I'd rather like to talk to you about those fascinating circuits you left with me.'

At the door of his private elevator in the foyer, Vaughn turned to his Deputy. 'Packer, be so good as to see what progress Professor Watkins is making,' he purred. 'You might even offer him a little gentle encouragement.' Then he ushered his visitors up to the top floor.

As they walked into the spacious, functional office Jamie whistled in astonishment. 'It's just like your London office,' he exclaimed.

Vaughn chuckled amiably. 'Confusing, isn't it?' He motioned them to sit down in the stylish chairs facing his desk. 'It's the secret of my success, Doctor - standardisation and uniformity.'

'Mass production,' remarked the Doctor with obvious distaste.

Jamie hovered by the huge window, staring down between the vertical louvres at the complex of large factory buildings spread below. Steam and smoke rose everywhere and a distant humming sounded constantly.

'The essence of efficiency, Doctor.' Vaughn said expansively.

The Doctor smiled blandly back at him, giving nothing away.

'I should be angry with you both,' Vaughn went on. 'You have thwarted my security system twice. Why?'

The Doctor shrugged casually. 'It's quite simple, Mr Vaughn. I detest computers and I refuse to be controlled by them.'

'Your young friend Zoe appears to feel the same. She completely destroyed one of our reception installations.'

Jamie spun round. 'So that's why your bully boys got hold of her and Isobel,' he blurted out.

Vaughn turned to him with an offended smile. 'My dear young man, on the contrary I found the incident quite amusing. She's a remarkable girl,' he turned back to the Doctor. 'And you, Doctor, are a remarkable man.'

The Doctor blushed. 'Why do you say that?' he inquired modestly.

Vaughn took the two circuit panels from the TARDIS from his inner pocket and laid them on the desk. 'Our Research Department found these baffling. Their structure seems totally illogical. Did you invent them yourself?'

The Doctor remained enigmatically silent.

Vaughn stood up, cleverly concealing his frustration. 'So you are determined to preserve your secrets, Doctor. I can hardly blame you. We shall do all we can to help.'

The Doctor inclined his head. 'You're very kind.'

Vaughn walked over to his private elevator. 'Please make yourselves at home,' he said graciously.'I will see if I can personally persuade Professor Watkins to divert his talents to investigating your little problem.'

As soon as he had gone, Jamie rushed over to the Doctor. 'What aboot Zoe and Isobel?' he cried.

'Don't worry. I haven't forgotten them,' the Doctor assured him.

'Och, I know they were in those box things, Doctor.'

The Doctor held up his hands patiently. 'Jamie, we won't help the girls by annoying Mr Vaughn,' he warned him.

'But he's being nice as pie to us.'

'Too nice, Jamie.' The Doctor picked up the circuits. 'And he's a little too interested in these for my liking.'

Jamie's eyes widened. 'Do ye think he knows aboot the TARDIS, Doctor?' he whispered.

'I don't see how he could.'

Jamie went back over to the panoramic window 'Och well, perhaps the Professor will be able to tell us what's happening here.'

The Doctor bit his lip and sighed. 'That's what puzzles me, Jamie. If Vaughn has anything to hide, why is he going to allow us to see Watkins?'

In a cluttered room in the basement below the building, Packer was lounging against the wall staring with sneering contempt at a short stout balding man of about sixty clad in baggy trousers, rolled-up shirtsleeves and an unbuttoned waistcoat. The bearded little man gazed back at Packer with undisguised loathing through thick wire-framed spectacles. Electronic circuitry and tangles of cable were scattered over a large bench and even over the crude unmade bunk in one corner.

'She's a pretty girl, your niece,' Packer was saying casually. 'It'd be such a shame to spoil her.'

'You're a pathetic little sadist, Packer,' Professor Watkins retorted sadly. 'I don't believe you anyway.'

Packer stepped towards him, eyes blazing. 'You know I don't make idle threats. If you value the girl you'll do as Mr Vaughn wishes.'

Watkins snorted. 'Assuming you really have got Isobel, how do I know you haven't harmed her already?'

At that moment Vaughn appeared in the doorway. 'You can take my word for that, Professor,' he announced soothingly.

Watkins turned sharply, squinting through his pebble lenses. 'Your word!' he scoffed dismissively.

Vaughn strolled across to the bench and frowned at a complicated assemblage of partially connected cathode tubes, transistors and coils almost buried within a web of tiny coloured wires. 'So you still haven't completed the device . . .' he scolded menacingly.

'No. I don't intend to complete it,' snapped Watkins.

Vaughn swung round on the trembling little figure. 'Oh, I think you will, Professor,' he purred. 'Otherwise, much as I abhore violence, I might not be able to restrain Packer's enthusiasm for persuasive hospitality. The choice is yours.'

Shaking with outrage, Watkins brazened it out for a few more seconds. Finally he slumped meekly in defeat. 'You'll let the poor child go if I cooperate?' he muttered faintly.

'No, no, no... She is our guarantee,' Vaughn protested indignantly. 'But she'll come to no harm.'

Watkins blinked at his smiling tormentors in anguish. 'Very well,' he conceded at last. 'But I want to see Isobel first.'

'Of course you do,' Vaughn agreed. 'However, one more thing.'

The Professor started suspiciously and retreated a few paces.

'Some friends of yours are here and they're determined to see you,' Vaughn informed his victim.

Watkins frowned. 'Friends? I'm not allowed visitors,' he retorted. 'I might tell them everything!'

Vaughn threw back his distinguished head and laughed. 'You know nothing to compromise me. Besides, Professor, don't forget Isobel.'

Packer thrust his pale perspiring face at Watkins. 'Because *I* certainly shan't forget Isobel,' he threatened, baring his discoloured teeth.

The Professor hesitated for a moment, then bowing to the inevitable, he turned reluctantly to his half-assembled apparatus and sighed, shaking his domed head in distress.

Vaughn paused in the doorway. 'Conduct the Professor's visitors down to him, Packer,' he ordered benignly and walked out.

In Vaughn's office, Jamie and the Doctor were at the window and Jamie was pointing out a strange building he had noticed in the distance. The Doctor fished out a small brass telescope and extended it. 'My goodness me!' he muttered, focussing on the three large spheres mounted on the roof of a small windowless building on the far side of the complex. 'It looks like a deep space communications installation, Jamie.'

'What's it doing here, Doctor?'

The Doctor shrugged. 'The plot thickens...' he murmured, studying the structure carefully.

Suddenly Jamie pointed to a tiny black shape high

above the distant woodland. 'A helicopter! Perhaps it's the Brigadier's mob,' he whispered.

Before the Doctor could refocus the telescope the door slid open and Packer swaggered in. 'Come with me,' he snapped malevolently.

The Doctor turned and stared at him with raised eyebrows.

Packer stared back, thrilled at the prospect of trouble. But the Doctor's steadfast gaze eventually disconcerted him and at last he got the message. 'Please, gentlemen . . .' he added through clenched teeth.

With a brilliant smile, the Doctor led Jamie to the door.

As soon as he was alone with his visitors Professor Watkins seemed to conquer his profound suspicion and to relax a little. 'Of course . . . Anne Travers told me all about you, Doctor,' he beamed. 'She was a brilliant student.'

'Indeed. They're in America now, I believe,' replied the Doctor, his eyes shifting surreptitiously around the jumbled room while they chatted.

'But what are you doing here?' Watkins inquired brightly.

The Doctor coughed and blew his nose loudly. 'That's rather a long story.' he murmured confidentially. 'But the fact is, I need help with some faulty circuits out of the TARDIS.'

Watkins looked puzzled. Then he nodded and smiled. 'Ah yes . . . your machine. I remember Anne's description was most intriguing. I'd like to hear more . . .'

Again the Doctor coughed and then blew his nose violently. 'I fear Miss Travers may have allowed her imagination to run rather wild,' he replied, weaving his way through the disorder towards the Professor's bunk.

Watkins's eager face clouded with disappointment. 'You mean the travel machine doesn't exist?' he cried.

'Och, of course it does,' Jamie burst out, 'we landed in it this morning not far from . . .'

His words were muffled by a prolonged fit of wheezing and coughing from the Doctor who was now perched on the bunk facing them and shooting significant glances towards a small ventilator grille set into the wall.

Then Jamie noticed something glinting in one corner of the grille. 'Och ... Aye ...' he mumbled shamefacedly, turning to the Professor and mouthing a frantic warning.

Professor Watkins glanced from one to the other, utterly confused by their extraordinary antics. 'Are you all right?' he ventured kindly.

'Never felt better!' the Doctor laughed, starting to rummage feverishly in his many bulging pockets. 'Tell us something about your important work here, Professor,' he suggested with exaggerated enthusiasm.

'My work?' Watkins echoed with flattered delight. 'Oh, it's really just a new kind of teaching aid ...'

The Doctor nodded energetically, grimacing as if to encourage Watkins to keep talking regardless.

At last the Professor's feeble eyesight made out the miniature television camera lens fitted inside the grille. 'It's ... it's called a Cerebration Mentor,' he burbled on. 'It is able to transmit encoded thought patterns directly into the brain ... However the device can also induce emotional changes in the subject and therefore make it more susceptible to rapid learning ...'

At that moment the Doctor found what he wanted. It was a small but exceedingly powerful magnet. 'Most ingenious, Professor,' he exclaimed, reaching up and attaching the magnet to the grille right next to the lens. 'But not foolproof, I'm afraid!'

Tobias Vaughn's faintly amused smile abruptly vanished as the image on the monitor broke up, flashed violently and disappeared.

'Check the system,' he snapped.

Packer hastily pressed several buttons on the Director's desk. At once the other eight video screens all showed clear, slowly scanning views of various sections of the complex.

Vaughn turned sharply away from the bank of screens, flushing with pent up frustration. 'Our friend, the Doctor, is a resourceful man. No wonder our allies fear him,' he grunted, staring across at the blank wall.

Packer's scalp crept visibly in surprise. 'They know him?'

'They encountered him on another planet.'

Packer's small but prominent eyeballs bulged. 'That's impossible.'

'No, Packer. The Doctor operates some kind of travel device. The barbarian Scottish youth confirmed it a moment ago. Our allies ordered me to destroy the Doctor, but first I must discover the secrets of this extraordinary machine.'

Packer's face suddenly betrayed a deeply rooted unease. He licked his thin lips nervously. 'But if you were ordered to . . .'

Vaughn thumped the desk decisively. 'I don't take orders, Packer, I give them,' he shouted, striding across to the elevator. 'The time has come to stop playing cat and mouse with the Doctor and his friends.'

4

Hitching Lifts

Professor Watkins shuffled slowly round his basement prison wringing his gnarled hands in desperation. 'If Vaughn has your young friend Zoe as well as Isobel then we are completely at his mercy,' he submitted.

'Not entirely. There is still the Brigadier remember,' the Doctor pointed out. 'But quickly, Professor, we have little time. What do you know about Vaughn's activities? What's he up to here?'

Watkins fluttered his hands helplessly. 'I know no more than you do Doctor, except that he wants control of my invention to add to his electronics empire.'

The Doctor sighed. 'I've a nasty feeling he's aiming a lot higher than that, my dear fellow.'

'Someone's coming!' Jamie warned them, retreating from the door where he'd been keeping watch.

The Doctor hurried across to the ventilator and was just about to remove his magnet from the grille when Vaughn strode in with Packer sneering at his elbow.

'Please don't trouble yourself, Doctor... allow me,' Vaughn smiled, going over and removing the magnet. He held the tiny object aloft like a trophy. 'Most ingenious... but alas not foolproof,' he joked.

The Doctor bowed, acknowledging the irony of the situation.

Vaughn's bland manner abruptly changed, becoming cold and undisguised. 'You must realise that you force me to consider other methods of obtaining the information I want.'

Inwardly boiling with resentment and rage, the Doctor

remained silent and impassive. Jamie's fists clenched and unclenched behind his back.

'Your friend Zoe will arrive here shortly...' Vaughn began.

'So you *have* got the lassie,' Jamie shouted, barging forward. 'If ye've harmed her...'

Vaughn waved him away disdainfully. 'Doctor, I want your travel machine,' he announced curtly. 'Either you hand it over to me or Packer will be obliged to introduce Miss Zoe to his rather crude form of hospitality. You have exactly sixty minutes to decide. Packer!'

The gleam of anticipation shone in Packer's beady eyes as he drew his pistol and motioned the Doctor and Jamie towards the door. The Doctor grasped Jamie firmly by the arm and guided him to obey.

As Packer marched them outside, Vaughn wandered over to the cowering figure by the bench. 'No more interruptions, Professor,' he promised, with a bleak smile. 'And now I suggest that you continue with your vital work.'

Under Vaughn's pale gaze, Watkins picked up a soldering probe and bowed half-heartedly over his apparatus to resume his thankless task with trembling hands.

Meanwhile, Packer escorted his prisoners to the main elevator shaft and summoned the lift. As they waited, the Doctor stared up at the indicator and suddenly shivered.

'What's wrong?' asked Jamie.

'Just my little phobia about lifts,' the Doctor shrugged, grinning wanly at Packer. Then he turned to Jamie and swivelled his eyes and contorted his eyebrows in a brief pantomime of signals.

After a baffled pause Jamie nodded furiously. 'Och aye, Doctor... Yer wee phobia?' he murmured sympathetically.

As the lift arrived and the doors slid open the Doctor suddenly turned to Packer and gave a hopeless shrug. 'It's no good Mr Packer, I can't bear to let Zoe suffer,' he admitted. 'I'd better tell you what you want to know.'

Packer's bloodless mouth compressed with suspicion and he raised his gun. 'You're willing to talk?' he demanded, sensing his opportunity to redeem himself in Vaughn's estimation.

The Doctor nodded, nudging Jamie to enter the lift. 'Actually I'd rather tell *you* everything...' he continued, frantically gesturing to Jamie behind his back. 'I find Mr Vaughn rather . . .' The Doctor stared deliberately over Packer's shoulder. 'Too late. Here he comes now,' he muttered, backing into the lift as Packer turned to look down the empty corridor.

Meanwhile Jamie had pressed a button and the doors started to close before Packer could turn back to them. The Doctor just managed to wriggle between the doors in time. They snapped together and the lift began to ascend.

'Quick, give me your dirk,' he cried.

Jamie reached into his sock and drew out a short, wicked-looking dagger. Snatching it eagerly the Doctor prised the faceplate off the control panel and yanked out a handful of wires.

'What are ye doing?' Jamie gasped in alarm.

The Doctor gave the bundle of wires a sharp tug. 'We shall either stop or crash back down the shaft,' he announced impassively.

Jamie glanced at the floor indicator. 'But we're six floors up!' he shrieked.

'Then hold tight,' muttered the Doctor, tugging again.

There was a short burst of sparks and a few wisps of black smoke from the panel and the lift whined to a halt. They held their breaths. Suddenly there was a scream of distant gears and the lift dropped several metres before jerking to a stop again.

White-faced and sweating they picked themselves up off the floor. Jamie gazed in disbelief as the Doctor gingerly bounced up and down a few times. To their relief the lift stayed put.

The Doctor grinned. 'It was a fifty-fifty chance, Jamie, but we're safe,' he said smugly.

'We're not. We're stuck five floors up!' Jamie protested

heatedly, snatching back his dirk and shoving it down his sock.

The Doctor smiled patiently. 'Jamie, the lift is stuck, not us,' he retorted, pointing up at the small trapdoor in the ceiling above them. 'Come on, up you go.'

The Doctor touched his toes and Jamie clambered reluctantly onto his back. 'Och, ye're a clever wee chap,' he admitted grudgingly, pushing open the trapdoor.

'Thank you, Jamie,' came the Doctor's muffled response, 'and you're a brave wee chap, so you can go first.'

A few minutes later Jamie had heaved the Doctor up through the hatchway and they crouched on the roof of the lift, gazing apprehensively up the long shaft where the greasy cables disappeared into the darkness.

The Doctor tested the narrow steel ladder clamped to the wall of the shaft. 'It's a long climb, Jamie, but with luck we'll reach the top before they realise what's happened.' Something scribbled in the thick layer of dust on the lift roof caught his eye. 'Who's Kilroy?' he wondered absently.

Jamie grinned and wiped his finger. 'Och, nobody you'd know. Come on, Doctor.'

With Jamie leading the way they started to climb the vertical ladder, their laboured efforts causing eerie echoes in the tall dark shaft.

'Doctor, what happens if... if they get the lift working again before... we reach the top?' panted Jamie after a while.

The Doctor grunted breathlessly. 'Quite simple, Jamie. We get squashed...'

Jamie smiled grimly to himself at the epitaph they had left below them in the dust... KILROY WAS HERE.

Vaughn stood by the elevator doors shaking his head incredulously.

'I'll kill them...' spluttered Packer, his hand over the mouthpiece of the service telephone.

'You'll do no such thing,' Vaughn snapped. 'I want

them alive.'

'What the hell happened?' Packer yelled down the phone. 'Well, use the emergency circuits, man,' he ordered, slamming the receiver down. 'The thing's stuck between the fourth and fifth floors.'

'So I gathered, Packer,' murmured Vaughn ominously. 'Our clever Doctor has outwitted you once again.'

Packer's cruel mouth twitched and curled with hatred. 'Well, now he's been a bit too clever. He's trapped,' he sneered.

Vaughn's face darkened. 'I don't understand his motive,' he pondered, 'Unless he's just playing for time.'

Packer seized the receiver and punched a few digits with his gloved knuckle. 'Packer. Cover all lift doors. Two men on each floor. Now. Move,' he rapped.

Vaughn shaded his eyes, his sensibilities offended by his Deputy's hysterical behaviour. 'Calm down, Packer, our birds can't fly away,' he protested quietly.

They waited, Vaughn expressionless and unblinking, Packer tense and fidgetting. Eventually the service telephone buzzed. Packer answered.

'Right. Send it down to the basement,' he instructed.

Two armed and visored security guards came clattering down the concrete emergency stairs next to the elevator shaft just as the indicator light lit up. They levelled their machine pistols as the lift doors opened.

Packer stared open-mouthed into the empty car. 'They've vanished... just vanished!' he whined. 'Did it stop anywhere on the way down?' he rapped into the telephone. 'No? You sure?' he demanded shrilly.

'Come here, Packer,' Vaughn called wearily from inside the lift.

Dry-throated and sweating, Packer obeyed. Vaughn was pointing to the trapdoor. Packer's eyes narrowed to slits of glittering malice.

'I'll get them, sir... I'll get them,' Packer vowed, dabbing his cheese-coloured forehead with his sleeve.

'Call me when you do. I'll be in my office,' Vaughn ordered, walking despairingly out of the lift. 'And try not to lose them...'

Smarting from his master's sarcastic taunt in front of the two guards, Packer pulled back his cuff and viciously spat orders into his miniature radio. 'Packer. They're in the shaft. Get men onto the roof immediately.' He hesitated a moment, his nose slowly puckering into a sneer of malicious anticipation. 'And tell the engineer to take the lift right to the top. Now!' he added, beckoning the two guards into the car with him.

Furiously clambering up through the dusty, greasy darkness, Jamie and the Doctor desperately redoubled their efforts when they heard the terrifying clanks and whirrings as the lift became operational again and the cables started whipping and clattering only a few centimetres away from them. Above them the electric motor whined inexorably and below them the grinding of wheels and the shrieking of bearings rose relentlessly towards them.

'Quick, Jamie... Quick...' the Doctor gasped feebly from the rickety ladder beneath him. 'It's catching us up.'

At last Jamie reached the metal gantry supporting the winding gear. 'McCrimmons for ever...' he whooped, wrenching open the steel door in the concrete housing and bursting onto the flat roof. The Doctor struggled out after him and they lay on their backs for a few seconds, gratefully gulping the cool fresh air. Suddenly the harsh whining ceased abruptly and there was a final numbing clang as the lift hit its buffer-stops, sending a red-hot shiver through their exhausted bodies.

Then the Doctor jumped up. 'Come on, Jamie,' he panted, stumbling across to the parapet and looking over the edge at the dizzying drop below.

'Och, just a wee minute...' Jamie pleaded, moaning with fatigue.

'No time to lose,' yelled the Doctor, climbing over the parapet and disappearing.

Jamie sat bolt upright, a stifled scream blocking his throat. Dumb with horror, he limped across the roof, scarcely daring to look down. To his relief he saw that the

Doctor was running down a fire-escape fitted in the angle of the L-shaped building.

'Come on, Jamie, they'll be up there any minute.'

Jamie shut his eyes and dragged himself over the parapet. As he started slithering down the metal staircase a blood-curdling chorus of howling sirens broke out all around the complex...

Packer stood dejectedly in front of Vaughn's desk, his uniform torn and his face streaked with dirt. 'They must have gone down the fire escape, sir...' he mumbled, concluding his pathetic report.

Vaughn shook his head very, very slowly, rising to his feet and gazing out over his empire spread before him. Suddenly he punched a fist into his open palm and rounded on his Deputy. 'I want the Doctor and the boy,' he said in an awful, hushed voice.

There was silence. Then Packer swallowed. 'The whole compound's on alert, sir. It's only a matter of time.'

Vaughn uttered a short derisive laugh.

Packer's bottled up frustration suddenly erupted. 'You should have let me deal with them properly right at the start,' he snarled accusingly. 'And if you'd only obey our allies' orders...'

'Orders, Packer?' Vaughn echoed, moving up to him. 'I told you before; I don't obey orders, I give them.'

Packer stared at him like a mesmerised animal. 'But you can't fight *them*!' he spluttered.

Vaughn smiled blandly. 'The invasion will be under my control and when it is successfully accomplished I shall remain supreme,' he declared confidently. 'Why do you suppose I keep that senile old fool Watkins alive?'

'To work on his machine.'

'Our allies are extremely disturbed by the Professor's machine,' Vaughn revealed. 'They ordered me to destroy the prototype.'

Packer gazed at his Director in astonishment. 'They are afraid of it?'

'Oh, its teaching function doesn't worry them, but when

we generated some emotion pulses...' Vaughn paused dramatically, savouring Packer's bewilderment. 'I am convinced that the emotional pulses could be used to destroy our allies,' he concluded.

Packer looked thoroughly rattled. 'That's just a guess,' he muttered.

Vaughn shook his head slyly. 'No, it's a reasonable gamble,' he argued, 'and we're playing for very high stakes, are we not?'

Packer licked his tacky lips. 'You're taking too big a chance,' he croaked.

Vaughn moved even closer to him, his pale eyes boring like lasers. 'Do you want to be totally converted, Packer?' he whispered hoarsely. 'Do you want to become inhuman? One of them?'

Packer tried to step back but his legs were like jelly.

Vaughn pursued his fear relentlessly. 'That's what will happen to us if they take over. We shall cease to be human. However, we can make use of their force to conquer the world and then discard them at our leisure,' he proposed, as casually as if he were describing a parlour game.

After a pause Packer grinned faintly. 'You're sure Watkins's device can do it?'

Vaughn shrugged indifferently. 'If we obtain the Doctor's travel machine we can escape if necessary.'

'Insurance?'

'Precisely, Packer,' Vaughn grinned, patting his arm. 'And speaking of insurance, have the two girls arrived?'

Packer informed him that they should be on their way over to the Administration Building.

'Excellent,' Vaughn approved. 'When they are safely tucked away we shall flush out our clever Doctor.'

All at once a high-pitched bleeping sounded from Packer's wrist. He held the minute radio to his ear. As he listened, his face quickly twisted with apprehension and anger.

'There's an unidentified helicopter in the area and Perimeter Security report strangers sighted near the compound,' he informed his master, shifting uneasily in anticipation of Vaughn's reaction. 'I think the Doctor may be connected to the UNIT organisation. What are we going to do, sir?'

Vaughn went to the window and scanned the skies. 'Nothing,' he snapped.

Packer was astounded. 'Nothing at all, sir?'

'They cannot hurt us, Packer,' Vaughn assured him in an almost unnatural voice. 'Just leave this to me...'

Thanks to their memory of the layout of the complex seen from Vaughn's office window, Jamie and the Doctor managed to reach the railway sidings very quickly without being spotted. They shut themselves inside a freight wagon and flopped down between the containers to recover their breath. All around them sirens droned their eerie alert and they soon heard the tramping of boots outside as Packer's men searched the yard.

'D'ye think this could be the train Zoe and Isobel were on?' Jamie whispered.

The Doctor considered a moment. 'If it is then these crates should be empty, Jamie.'

Jamie knelt up. 'Soon see,' he grunted, heaving at the lid of the nearest container. Slowly it swung open. He could just distinguish a bulky outline in a kind of plastic material surrounded by dense cobweb filaments, like a cocoon lying in the darkness. 'Och, these are full,' he said, disappointed.

The Doctor crawled over and peered into the crate. His face went rigid and he bit his lip uncertainly. 'I wonder what it is...'

Sudden voices outside silenced him. 'Search these wagons!' someone shouted and they heard the ominous sound of wagon doors opening.

'Quick, Jamie, hide,' warned the Doctor, jamming himself into a tiny niche between the stacks of containers.

Jamie searched around feverishly for somewhere for himself. All at once the handle of the door was wrenched back and the heavy door started to slide open. In sheer desperation Jamie clambered into the open container and pulled down the lid in the nick of time. There was just room for him squeezed betwen the lid and the strange object underneath. He lay motionless, scracely breathing while the guards searched the wagon.

Suddenly he felt a slight movement beneath him and heard a faint brittle rustling, like dead leaves in a breeze. Instantly a clammy cold sweat broke out all over his body and tiny hot needles seemed to prick his neck and scalp. He fought to stifle a scream of terror and the urge to jump out of the crate. In the end he hardly knew whether it was his own quaking or something else that was really moving underneath him. The nightmare seemed eternal, but eventually he heard the wagon door slide shut and all was quiet again.

The Doctor crept out and opened the lid.

'Doctor...'

'Ssssh, Jamie, the guards are still outside.'

Jamie climbed out, his teeth chattering with fright. 'That thing in there... it moved!' he whispered.

The Doctor stared at the cocoon thing and shook his head. 'Imagination, Jamie. Darkness plays strange tricks.'

'But I *felt* it, Doctor.'

The Doctor looked sceptical. 'Are you sure? Then we'd better take a look.'

At that moment there was a commotion outside. Sangster and Graves, get those girls over to Administration pronto...' someone shouted.

'The lassies!' Jamie hissed, forgetting the horror of the last few minutes and making for the door.

The Doctor grabbed his sleeve. 'Wait, Jamie. Let things quieten down out there, then we'll go and find them.'

Reluctantly Jamie obeyed, but his blood was up and his blue eyes sparkled with aggressive determination.

As soon as the guards had gone, they emerged cautiously from the freight wagon and then sprinted hell-for-leather along the narrow alleyways between the huge factory buildings towards the Administration Block. The sirens had stopped wailing, but they had to dodge and dive for cover whenever patrols or personnel appeared. Eventually they rounded a corner of the generating plant and flattened themselves behind an empty skip to watch

Packer supervising the opening of two containers which had just been deposited on the steps of the entrance to the Administration Building by a small forklift truck.

Zoe and Isobel were hauled roughly out of the crates and bundled through the glass doors at the base of the tower. Jamie and the Doctor just managed to overhear Packer order the girls to be taken up to the tenth floor. While the Doctor twiddled his thumbs with profound concentration, working out a way to get to the prisoners, Jamie screwed up his eyes and watched a helicopter chattering across the sky some distance away from the complex.

'Must be some of the Brigadier's mob, Doctor. Let's call him up,' he suggested impatiently.

But the Doctor said that it was too soon for that. First they must rescue Zoe and Isobel. And as soon as the coast was clear, he led Jamie in a desperate sprint across the open concrete yard and round to the back of the tower. 'Sorry, Jamie, but I'm afraid I abhor lifts . . .' he grinned, leading the way back up the fire-escape in the angle between the tower and the adjoining buildings.

Gritting his teeth, Jamie scowled and clambered reluctantly up the metal spiral behind him.

Inside the busy, cramped Operations Room, Lethbridge-Stewart stirred a fresh mug of tea as he listened intently to Captain Turner's muffled report from the helicopter.

'Lot of unusual activity down in the compound, sir. Looks like some kind of alert.'

'Any sign of the Doctor and the boy?'

'None, sir.'

The Brigadier nibbled thoughtfully at a digestive biscuit. 'Right, Jimmy. Pull out and stand by,' he ordered crisply.

He swung round in his chair and studied the Situation Map for a few minutes, tugging the ends of his moustache. 'All units please,' he requested.

The Signals Sergeant flicked a bank of switches. 'Go ahead, sir.'

The Brigadier picked up his handset. 'Lethbridge-

Stewart to all Red units. Penetration of Red Sector imminent. Report readiness.'

He dunked the remains of the biscuit impatiently while he waited for the situation reports. It fell apart and floated on the top.

'Red Victor One mustering to standby. Ten minutes, sir... Red Victor Two standing by, sir... Red Victor Three...'

As the brisk responses buzzed in his ear the Brigadier picked up his beret, breathed on the UNIT badge and proudly polished it against his chest. 'Right, Doctor. We're ready when you are,' he murmured.

At that moment, the Doctor was leading Jamie precariously along a narrow ledge leading from one of the landings on the fire-escape to a vertical maintenance ladder which ran up the side of the connecting building, linking the step-like series of flat roofs at the rear of the Administration Building. They shinned recklessly up the shuddering rungs to the first roof and dropped down behind the parapet to rest a moment.

'That'll be the tenth floor up there,' gasped the Doctor, pointing to the sheer wall of glass rising like a cliff above the next roof.

Jamie craned upwards unenthusiastically. 'Aye, but how do we ken which room they're in?' he objected. 'And how do we get them out?'

'Stop looking for problems,' the Doctor snapped. 'Let's just get up there first, Jamie.' He scurried across the asphalt and started scrambling up the vertical ladder to the next storey.

Just as Jamie followed suit, Vaughn's eerily calm voice suddenly blared out from huge tannoy speakers fixed to the corners of the tower building above them:

'Wherever you are, Doctor, listen carefully. You have just ten minutes to relinquish your freedom. Ten minutes from now your friend Zoe will pay for your foolish lack of cooperation...'

Clinging unsteadily to the creaking ladder, they listened

to the cold mechanical threat echoing around the complex.

'Not much time,' muttered Jamie gloomily, staring up at the inaccessible identical windows.

'Oh, time enough to effect a simple rescue operation,' replied the Doctor with airy confidence. 'Come on, Jamie.'

Seconds later they reached the second roof and Jamie suddenly grabbed the Doctor's arm and pointed upwards. 'Somebody's there. It's Zoe!' he cried excitedly.

While Jamie started waving frantically to attract the attention of the vague figure behind the reflective glass ten or so metres above them, the Doctor took out the polyvox unit the Brigadier had given him, deployed the stubby aerial and pressed the call button. 'Jamie, try to tell Zoe to keep away from the window, otherwise she'll give the game away,' he muttered urgently. 'And keep down.'

'Hallo Doctor, come in . . .' buzzed the Brigadier.

'Brigadier, I think we shall require your assistance in a few minutes. Do you have a helicopter in the vicinity?' said the Doctor hurriedly.

'We do indeed, Doctor.'

'Equipped with a rope ladder of some kind?'

'Naturally, Doctor. I'll order Captain Turner to find you immediately.'

The Doctor glanced up at the roof of the Administration Building a dozen storeys above them. 'We'll be on the roof of the tower block, Brigadier. North East corner. That should give your helicopter cover from any ground fire.'

'Excellent,' crackled the Brigadier appreciatively. 'Over and out.'

'Oh yes . . . Out and . . . and about,' the Doctor signed off, trying to hide his uneasy expression from Jamie as he stared at the thin metal ladder running up the side of the tower. 'And all in one piece too, I trust!'

Zoe had been staring down at the grey concrete and metal buildings which formed the International Electromatix Factory Complex with an expression of hopeless gloom. 'I'm sorry, Isobel, this is all my fault,' she muttered. 'If I hadn't blown up that stupid computer...'

Isobel still looked shocked after the ordeal inside the containers. 'Why didn't they just turn us over to the fuzz or something, Zoe?' she wondered. 'It was horrible inside those crate things. Why have they kidnapped us like this?'

Zoe shrugged. 'I don't see any way out of here, Isobel. It's a sheer drop,' she said, turning to look round the bare featureless office where they were imprisoned. 'There's nothing to make any sort of ladder with either.'

'Or a set of wings,' Isobel joked with a brave smile, pressing her pale face to the window. Suddenly she caught sight of Jamie waving frantically directly below them. 'Zoe, look, it's Jamie and the Doctor!' she cried, clapping her hands with delight.

Zoe peered down, trying to interpret Jamie's wild gestures. 'I think Jamie's telling us to keep away from the window, Isobel.'

Jamie was pointing to his eyes and then to the window and then doing an obscure little mime.

The two girls glanced at each other in bewilderment. Then Zoe noticed that what appeared to be a spotlight bulb suspended from the ceiling was in fact a rotatable electronic eye.

'Just act as if nothing was happening...' she murmured out of the side of her mouth. 'I think Big Brother is watching us.'

They moved away from the window with affected casualness and sat down against the wall, as if giving up all thought of resistance. But inside, they were tense with excitement and expectation.

Vaughn pressed a button on his desk and leaned towards the slim microphone. 'Doctor, you have just five minutes left,' he announced in an expressionless monotone. 'Do you hear me, Doctor? Five minutes...'

Packer stood at the window, listening to his miniature VHF unit and scanning the sky over the complex. 'They won't give themselves up, Mr Vaughn. They'd be mad to,' he whined.

'Not mad, Packer. Merely human,' Vaughn retorted mildly, selecting a different channel on one of the video screens in the wall opposite him. 'They won't want their charming little friends to come to any harm.'

On the screen, Zoe and Isobel appeared sitting in disconsolate silence on the floor of their room. Packer turned and gazed at them, his lip curling in a cruel sadistic sneer.

The sudden clattering whine of a helicopter made Packer spin round to the window again. 'The helicopter, Mr Vaughn. It's right overhead!' he warned.

For a fleeting moment Vaughn looked slightly uneasy. He came to the window and looked up at the helicopter as it passed out of sight, hovering directly over the tower block. Then he looked back at the girls slumped in their prison. 'Perhaps the Doctor and the boy plan to save their own skins and to desert the young ladies,' he speculated. 'How very ungallant of them. No doubt the helicopter is manoeuvering to pick them up. Stop them, Packer. Shoot the machine down if necessary.'

Packer's eyes lit up. 'Yes, Mr Vaughn!' he rapped and he hurried out of the office.

Vaughn reclined in his chair, observing the girls on the screens for a moment. Then he leaned forward and pressed the tannoy button. 'Two minutes, Doctor,' he murmured. 'Two mintues . . .'

Jamie was tempted to wrench the cables out of the speakers as he and the Doctor clambered over the parapet and onto the roof of the tower block with Vaughn's deafening warning ringing in their ears. He watched the Doctor signalling to Captain Turner to lower the rope ladder from the hovering helicopter.

'Surely you're not going to leave the lassies behind!' he shouted above the din of the rotors, as the end of the ladder came snaking down.

'Don't be an imbecile, Jamie,' the Doctor yelled back irritably, catching the swaying rungs and throwing them over the parapet on the side of the tower where Zoe and

Isobel were confined. He leaned over to check the length as Turner paid out the ladder from the helicopter. 'Good,' he muttered, signalling to Turner to stop lowering. 'Now Jamie, down you go.'

The beefy young Scot stared at him and then shuddered dizzily as he looked over the edge at the end of the ladder snapping to and fro in the stiff breeze. 'What? Me? Climb down there...?' he expostulated, backing away from the parapet.

'Surely you're not going to leave the lassies here?' the Doctor shouted sarcastically, punching Jamie's muscular arm.

Glaring resentfully, Jamie set his jaw, took a deep breath and hauled himself onto the violently swinging ladder and out over the parapet. As he began the long, terrifying climb down the lurching rungs, the banshee chorus of sirens struck up again, wailing the alert all over the compound.

Eventually Jamie reached the tenth floor and kicked himself sideways to align with the window where he had spotted Zoe.

The girls visibly jumped, screaming with fright as Jamie's heavy boots crashed against the glass. Zoe leaped to her feet and managed to force open one side of the window after a struggle.

'Come on, lassie, hurry yerself!' Jamie cried, squeezing himself through the gap and jumping into the room with the end of the ladder.

Isobel's delight at seeing him turned to queasy doubt. 'You... you don't expect us to climb up *that*, do you?' she exclaimed.

Jamie looked daggers at the pouting, countyish girl. 'Och, ye're quite welcome to stay here wi' Mr Packer,' he retorted indignantly.

Zoe gave Jamie a quick grateful hug. 'No, thanks,' she said firmly. 'Come on, Isobel.'

'Zoe first, then Isobel and me last,' Jamie commanded, steadying the ladder as Zoe obediently clambered on and started to climb confidently upwards. 'And dinna look down whatever ye do,' he added, lifting the trembling

Isobel onto the ladder with his free hand.

To Zoe and Isobel it seemed to take forever to reach the parapet where the Doctor was anxiously waiting for them under the threshing blades of the helicopter. Just as Zoe scrambled safely onto the roof a fusillade of machine pistol fire zipped up the side of the Administration Building from the main entrance far below, smashing several windows around Isobel. Jamie struggled desperately up the ladder behind her, shouting encouragement as bullets whizzed against the concrete and glass all around him. On the steps at the front of the building, Packer was screaming orders and gesticulating like a maniac up at his escaping quarry.

At last Isobel and Jamie were dragged unscathed over the parapet by Zoe and the Doctor.

'Thank goodness that's over...' gasped Isobel, ashen-faced.

'I'm afraid it isn't quite yet,' the Doctor shouted, pointing at the second length of ladder leading up at an angle to the helicopter hovering over the opposite corner of the rooftop.

Isobel shook her head in despair. 'I'm sorry. I don't think I can,' she panted.

Jamie put a comforting arm round her and squeezed. 'Course ye can, lassie.'

At that moment, a shower of lethal concrete splinters suddenly exploded out of the edge of the parapet, sending them all diving flat on their faces as Packer's men fired a last futile salvo at the roof.

Then Packer ordered his men onto the roof and stormed after them, seething with rage and frustration at his continuing failures.

With urgent persuasiveness, the Doctor, Zoe and Jamie finally got Isobel back onto the ladder. Zoe followed her, then the Doctor and finally Jamie. The ladder creaked and stretched under their combined weight and the rocking of the helicopter sent the fugitives gyrating in all directions.

Below them, Packer and his men were racing up the fire escape and as soon as they came within sight of the UNIT helicopter, they spread out over the flat roof immediately below the tower and concentrated their fire.

Safe in the helicopter, the Doctor, Zoe and Isobel yelled encouragement to Jamie as he forced himself up the last few rungs of the crazily whipping ladder with bullets sizzling past him. Four pairs of hands hauled him into the cabin and the pilot banked steeply and climbed rapidly away westwards and out of range.

5

Skeletons in Cupboards

Packer stood bowed and defeated in Vaughn's office, his lank hair sticking in long black strands across his sweating forehead.

'I told you so. That chopper was from the UNIT outfit. I told you . . .' he persisted accusingly.

His master was moving briskly around his desk, checking printouts and consulting telex messages.

'Oh, do stop panicking, Packer,' Vaughn purred wearily. 'Your incompetence defies description, but fortunately it no longer matters.'

Packer thumped the desk with both clenched fists. 'But there'll be an official reaction now that lot are involved,' he whined anxiously.

Vaughn clicked his tongue and shook his head. 'There will be no official reaction, Packer. I am fully in control of the situation, which is more than I can say for you.'

Packer muttered darkly to himself like a chided schoolboy.

'Don't argue!' Vaughn rapped. 'I want Watkins's Cerebration Machine loaded into the car immediately. We're going back to London.'

Packer stared at him aghast and started to object ineffectually.

Vaughn leaned forward on the desk and thrust his impassive face a few centimetres from his Deputy's pallid mask. 'Thanks to your bungling I shall be obliged to bring the invasion forward,' he murmured menacingly. 'We have just twenty-four hours to prepare.'

Packer looked appalled. Then he laughed derisively.

'Twenty-four hours? They'll never agree to that. The invasion forces are nowhere near complete . . .'

Vaughn silenced him with a curt nod. 'The forces are sufficient for our immediate purpose,' he hissed. 'You will attend to the machine and then bring Watkins up here to me. Meanwhile I shall attend to our UNIT friends.'

Packer opened his weak mouth to object, but the diamond glint in Vaughn's pale eye silenced him. Cowed, he turned on his heel and strode out with as much dignity as he could muster.

As soon as he was alone, Vaughn punched a private code into the keyboard of the small videophone in front of him. Seconds later, a smart young woman appeared on the screen.

'Good afternoon, Ministry of Defence.'

'Good afternoon, my dear. Major-General Routledge, please,' Vaughn requested pleasantly. 'My name is Tobias Vaughn.'

In the bowels of the vast Ministry of Defence building in Whitehall, Major-General Routledge sat in his cheerless, darkened office in front of an ornate marble fireplace with sporting trophies lining the mantelpiece. He was a thickset, square-faced man of about forty-five, with grey hair and moustache and a florid complexion. He was wearing a drab suit and a rugger club tie.

'. . . fine, Minister, I'll see you at eight at the Club. Goodbye,' he said into a green telephone receiver, laughing nervously as he rang off.

At once a light started flashing on the videophone unit mounted on the huge, cluttered mahogany desk. He pressed a switch and the smart young lady appeared.

'Outside call for you, General.'

Routledge cleared his throat and grinned roguishly at the screen. 'Male or female?' he inquired in a public school voice.

'Mr Tobias Vaughn, sir.'

Instantly Routledge's face set in an odd, uneasy half-smile and his eyes dulled imperceptibly. 'Vaughn? Ah yes . . . Mr Vaughn . . .' he stammered uncomfortably. 'Put him through on priority scramble.'

The screen fuzzed and then Vaughn's smiling face took shape. 'Good afternoon, Routledge. Is this channel secure?' he asked casually.

The Major-General nodded, croaking an indistinct confirmation.

'Excellent,' Vaughn replied, suddenly hardening his tone. 'Now listen to me. Your UNIT friends have been causing me considerable aggravation. They must be stopped at once. Do you understand?'

Routledge licked his pale lips and twisted his trembling hands together. 'I . . . I understand,' he mumbled after a pause. 'They must be stopped.'

Vaughn's eyes stared unblinkingly into his. 'There must be no more interference.'

'No more interference,' Routledge echoed meekly in a dreamy, mechanical voice. 'I shall deal with it at once.'

Vaughn smiled bleakly. 'Good fellow. I know I can rely on you,' he said with measured significance.

The screen went black and Routledge sat quite still staring at it for several minutes. Then he winced and sank his head into his hands and shuddered, slowly massaging his temples as if to rid himself of a violent headache. Eventually he gazed back at the screen again, his eyes glazed and lifeless. 'Yes. I understand,' he repeated, wiping his cold clammy forehead with his sleeve. 'UNIT must be stopped.'

The Brigadier was just cancelling the alert when Captain Turner ushered the exhausted Doctor and Jamie and their two rescued friends into the Hercules Operations Room.

'All Red Sector groups stand down and stand by,' he ordered briskly.

Then he jumped up to greet them heartily.

'Mission accomplished, sir,' Turner reported laconically.

'No casualities, Jimmy?'

'None, sir. Fortunately Vaughn's jackboot brigade can't

shoot for toffee.'

'Splendid!' breezed Lethbridge-Stewart, gesturing towards the welcoming tray of mugs of steaming tea and generously-filled sandwiches which an orderly was just bringing in.

Jamie grabbed a doorstep sandwich and started munching avidly. 'Aye, splendid. A simple rescue operation!' he muttered through his mouthful, glancing ironically at the Doctor who was nibbling thoughtfully on a more modest portion.

'But what about my uncle? He's still a prisoner,' Isobel pointed out anxiously, accepting a brimming mug of tea from Captain Turner.

'Don't worry, miss, I'm going to raise hell about this business and get some prompt action, I can tell you,' the Brigadier promised.

'If you'd had your camera with you, Isobel, you could have made a fortune with the pictures,' Zoe mused, sipping her tea gratefully.

'Yes. Pity, that would've clinched things as far as the Ministry is concerned,' agreed Turner.

The Brigadier frowned. 'Billy Routledge will have to take some action now. Not even Tobias Vaughn can get away with shooting at UNIT personnel,' he declared, indignantly stirring a heap of sugar into his tea.

The Doctor had not said a word. They all turned to him as he sat hunched over his untasted tea, chewing absently and staring into thin air.

Eventually Zoe broke the silence. 'What's the matter, Doctor?'

'Mmmm?' mumbled the Doctor distantly, still staring into space. 'Oh, I was just wondering, Zoe... That object we saw on the other side of the Moon this morning...'

Isobel exchanged looks of astonishment with the Captain and the Brigadier.

'Other side of the Moon?' spluttered the Brigadier, wiping his moustache.

'The TARDIS went wrong and we got stuck,' Jamie explained.

'And they fired a missile of some kind at us,' Zoe added.

'Who did?' demanded Captain Turner incredulously.

'Whoever it was in that spacecraft behind the Moon,' Zoe told him with patient emphasis.

'Spaceships behind the Moon?' exploded the Brigadier, blowing crumbs in all directions.

The Doctor gazed around the assembled throng of sceptical faces. 'There appears to be some kind of deep-space communications installation at Vaughn's factory complex...' he revealed quietly. 'And I am beginning to wonder...'

The Brigadier looked extremely disturbed at this revelation and he waited impatiently for the Doctor to continue.

Then Turner suddenly leaned over to his commanding officer. 'Sir, I know it sounds silly, but could those recent UFO reports have anything to do with all this?'

'Flying saucers?' Isobel exclaimed excitedly, nudging Zoe. 'Golly, what a scoop!'

The Doctor held up his hand for silence. 'Are there by any chance any photographs of the UFO sightings, Brigadier?' he asked eagerly.

'We've got quite a few in the files,' Lethbridge-Stewart replied, more worried than ever. 'Jimmy, would you fetch them?'

As the Captain hurried out, the Doctor dipped the remains of his sandwich into his neglected tea. 'Unidentified Flying Objects...' he ruminated, biting into the soggy mess, his eyes widening and his nostrils flaring with anticipation. 'Why didn't I think of that before...?'

Professor Watkins was in a state of nervous anxiety when Packer thrust him into Vaughn's office.

'What was all that shooting? Where is my niece? If you've hurt one hair of her head, Vaughn...' he babbled shrilly, blinking myopically at his tormentors.

'I assure you that Isobel is perfectly safe,' Vaughn purred blandly. 'At the moment anyway.'

Watkins struggled feebly in Packer's restraining grasp. 'I demand to see her!' he shouted.

Vaughn nodded and smiled. 'And so you shall, Professor. Just as soon as your machine is completed to my satisfaction.'

Watkins peered at him suspiciously. 'Why am I being taken back to London?'

Vaughn patted his arm affably. 'I am assigning Mr Gregory to work with you, Professor. You deserve some assistance with such an important assignment.'

'I don't need any assistance,' Watkins panted breathlessly.

'On the contrary,' Vaughn retorted calmly, 'you will have only twenty-four hours in which to complete the device to my specifications.'

The Professor shook his head violently. 'Never! Never!' he vowed defiantly.

Packer bent the Professor's podgy arm up behind his back and Watkins's plump body contorted with pain.

'If you cooperate, your niece will go free,' Vaughn promised. 'Otherwise . . .' He gestured ominously.

'You expect me to believe that?' Watkins scoffed.

Vaughn pointed to the bank of monitor screens behind his victim. Watkins turned and saw several still images of Isobel's frightened face staring out at him. Then Packer twisted his arm still further and shoved him brutally to his knees. Watkins knelt between them, moaning and whimpering helplessly.

Vaughn shrugged complacently. 'My dear Professor, you have no choice but to believe it,' he murmured silkily, his teeth flashing in the darkening room. He glanced distastefully at Packer but did not reprimand him for his excesses. Then he helped Watkins to his feet and smiled sympathetically. 'Now Professor, do please try and be sensible and do as I ask.'

In the UNIT Operations Room, the Doctor was poring intently over a microfilm viewer, studying a selection of remarkably clear pictures of various strange elongated hexagonal objects arranged in different formations.

The Brigadier peered hopefully over his shoulder.

'Mean anything to you, Doctor?' he asked after a prolonged silence.

The Doctor ran the film back and forth several times. 'Possibly, Brigadier. How long ago were these objects first sighted?' he murmured.

'Odd reports have trickled in for over a year, Doctor. We send fighters up to investigate, but no luck. Nothing.'

Captain Turner craned over the Doctor's other shoulder. 'The strange thing is they always seem to disappear somewhere over Northern Essex,' he remarked.

'That's where the International Electromatix manufacturing complex is!' Isobel exclaimed.

'Exactly,' said Turner, smiling at her.

The Doctor sat back, rubbing the side of his nose speculatively. 'Jamie, when you were hiding in the crate you said that whatever it was in there moved...'

Jamie shuddered at the vivid memory. 'Aye, Doctor. There's something wrapped up in all that plastic web stuff right enough.'

The Doctor meditated for a moment. 'Did you recognise anything about it, Jamie?'

'Och no, Doctor. It was far too dark and I was too scared,' Jamie admitted candidly.

The Doctor remained silent for a while, trying to visualise the vague shape they had seen in the crate inside the railway wagon.

'What do you think it was, Doctor?' asked Zoe in a hushed voice, remembering only too well her and Isobel's ordeal in the cramped, stuffy containers.

All at once the Doctor stood up abruptly, startling them. 'I'm not sure, Zoe, but I think we'd better find out as soon as possible.'

Jamie frowned. 'You mean, go back to Vaughn's place?' he cried in disbelief.

'Vaughn's obviously transporting the things from Essex to his London premises. That's where we'll find our answers,' the Doctor declared decisively. He asked the Brigadier if he had a map of the London set-up.

Lethbridge-Stewart looked disapprovingly at the bright-eyed little Time Lord. 'I don't think this is wise, Doctor.

You've just been very lucky so far.'

Jamie shoved his thumbs firmly in his belt. 'If you think I'm going back in there . . .' he snorted.

'We must find out what is in those containers,' the Doctor interrupted brusquely.

In the ensuing silence, Captain Turner pretended not to notice the Brigadier's critical gaze and he went over and selected a plastic map sheet from a rack beside the Situation Map. 'Here you are, Doctor, this shows the entire area in detail,' he said, handing it to the Doctor.

The Doctor beamed. 'Thank you, Captain.' He grinned at the Brigadier. 'Your staff are invaluable. Most efficient.' Then he began to examine the map carefully.

Slowly Jamie drew his thumbs out of his belt. Then he got up and went over to the Doctor. 'Och, we canna get in the same way again. They're sure to be on the lookout,' he muttered, becoming absorbed in the map.

The Doctor smiled secretively to himself, picked up a pen and started drawing on the back of his hand, consulting the map from time to time.

The Brigadier cleared his throat guiltily. 'Well, Doctor, anything I can do to help?' he inquired heartily.

The Doctor traced his finger along a thin wavering line on the plastic sheet. 'Yes, Brigadier, there is. Do you think you could possibly obtain a canoe for me?' he requested mysteriously.

An hour later, Jamie was sweating profusely and puffing away as he paddled the small canoe along a bleak stretch of stagnant canal running between tall derelict warehouses. In the stern the Doctor sat steering effortlessly with his paddle. Occasionally Jamie cast a resentful glance over his shoulder, but the Doctor always managed to appear to be doing his fair share of the work at the vital moment, grinning encouragingly at the toiling Scot. Frequently the Doctor studied the rough sketch he had drawn on the back of his hand and he hummed scraps of sea shanties to himself in a tone-deaf groan.

Suddenly they found themselves in pitch darkness as the

canal turned sharply and entered a long tunnel.

'Och, are ye sure ye ken where we are?' Jamie demanded doubtfully.

The Doctor hummed a few more bars, enjoying the added resonance the tunnel gave to his voice. 'Of course I do, Jamie. I know these waters like the back of my hand...' he giggled. 'We should be passing underneath Mr Vaughn's railway yards at this very moment.'

Cold, fetid water dripped on them and invisible fronds of clammy weed flapped in their faces from the tunnel roof. Jamie began to regret his decision to accompany the Doctor after all.

When they eventually emerged into the daylight again the Doctor steered towards a worn flight of slimy stone steps. 'These should lead into the back of the warehouse,' he whispered. 'Don't make a sound, Jamie.'

They tethered the canoe and cautiously climbed the treacherously slippery steps. Sure enough, they soon found themselves in a rubble-strewn yard behind the warehouse buildings. Two security guards with gauntlets and visors were visible in the distance where the railway lines entered the loading bay. Pressing themselves against the corrugated steel wall Jamie and the Doctor crouched down and made their way warily along the back of the huge warehouse, hoping that nobody would spot them before they managed to find a way inside.

They were lucky. Not far from the corner, they came upon an emergency exit. One of the doors was slightly ajar and by contorting his arm, Jamie was able to reach through the gap and jiggle the jammed releasing bar until it eventually freed itself. Cautiously he opened the door and they crept stealthily into the warehouse, dragging the door shut behind them.

As they slipped between the stacks of containers, they heard sounds of activity nearby. Creeping noiselessly from stack to stack they took care to avoid the prying electronic scanners ceaselessly panning to and fro from the roof girders. They soon reached a central area which was relatively clear except for a row of containers standing vertically on end, their lids open to reveal silvery cocoons like the one they had seen in the freight wagon earlier. Two men dressed in heavy protective suits with gloves and darkened visors were manoeuering a bulky apparatus mounted on wheels over to one of the open containers.

The Doctor stared keenly at the machine, the two lines running from his nose to the corners of his mouth deepening with grim concern. The apparatus consisted of a large central assemblage of tubes and wires topped by a curious corkscrew antenna; two thick umbilical cables led from the heart of the machine, ending in large crocodile clip connectors.

'Oh my goodness me,' the Doctor murmured, 'I was right.'

'What is it?' Jamie whispered.

'It looks like a multiphase bioprojector to me, Jamie.'

Jamie nodded, as if he were perfectly familiar with such things.

The two operatives had finished attaching the ends of the cables to the centre of the cocoon and they retreated behind a glass screen fitted to the apparatus and busied themselves with the complex array of controls and instruments. The antenna started rotating faster and faster, like a gigantic drill-bit. A low-pitched hum gradually filled the vast echoing building and rose relentlessly in pitch and intensity. A faint glow appeared inside the cocoon, growing stronger as the hum increased.

The Doctor drew Jamie further back behind the stacks of crates as the glow became a strobing glare which was almost intolerable to look at. A vaguely humanoid outline stirred inside the cocoon and a silver form began to flash with stronger and stronger pulses. Jamie and the Doctor covered their ears as the pulsating hum became an unbearable staccato shriek. In a sudden burst of thousands of silver fibres the cocoon exploded and a huge gleaming figure jerked spasmodically out of the crate, flashing and sparking.

Jamie went cold all over and his spine was tickled by a million icy needles. He gasped as the glittering giant strode forward trailing shreds of its chrysalis and breathing with a nightmarish mechanical rasp. He turned to the

Doctor as the overwhelming noise quickly died away and only the monster's heavy rhythmic breath disturbed the awed silence.

'Cybermen . . .!' he whispered, a tremor of disgust rippling through him as he recalled his brief encounter in the freight wagon.

With the Brigadier absent on an emergency visit to the Ministry of Defence, Zoe and Isobel were left in the Operations Room chatting to Captain Turner, while the other personnel absorbed themselves in their Taskforce duties.

'So what do you think will happen now?' asked Zoe.

'Well, it's not really a UNIT matter now,' Turner explained, 'so we'll probably hand it all over to the police.'

Isobel looked disappointed. 'Pity, I could've got some great pictures and made a bomb selling them to Fleet Street,' she brooded.

Turner shot her a flirtatious glance. 'Perhaps you'd allow me to make up for it by buying you dinner,' he suggested gallantly, eyeing Isobel's long shapely legs appreciatively.

Isobel looked delighted. 'Why not? Are you stinking rich or something?' she teased.

Turner laughed. 'Not on a Captain's pay, I'm not, but money isn't everything you know.'

Isobel considered his dark, handsome features. 'No, perhaps it isn't,' she agreed.

At that moment the door opened and Sergeant Walters brought in Jamie and the Doctor. They looked tired and drawn.

'What happened?' asked Zoe, eagerly running to meet them.

Jamie put his arm round her shoulder. 'Some auld friends of ours are back,' he murmured.

Slightly miffed by Turner's attentions to Isobel, Zoe put her arm affectionately round Jamie's waist. 'Oh, really?' she grinned. 'Who?'

'The Cybermen.'

Zoe looked appalled.

'I'm afraid there's no doubt about it,' the Doctor confirmed gloomily. 'I suspected as much some time ago, but I didn't want to cause unnecessary alarm, my dear.'

'What on earth are Cybermen?' demanded Isobel.

'Cybermen are inhuman killers from another galaxy,' the Doctor informed her gravely, sipping some leftover cold tea with a preoccupied air.

Captain Turner floundered out of his depth. 'You mean they're . . . well, they're from another world, Doctor?'

'That must have been their spacecraft on the other side of the Moon,' Zoe confided to Jamie.

Isobel giggled nervously. 'What exactly are they? Little green men?'

Only Turner smiled with her.

'I'm serious,' Zoe protested. 'We've met them before. They're fiendish, sadistic monsters.'

'Well . . . where exactly are they now?' Turner demanded, realising that the three intrepid strangers were in deadly earnest.

'They are being stockpiled at Vaughn's London headquarters,' replied the Doctor. 'There could be thousands of them.' He sat down, shaking his head.

'So Vaughn must be working with the Cyber Leaders . . .' Zoe concluded almost inaudibly.

The Doctor sighed and nibbled at a curled up sandwich. 'That deep-space communications installation Jamie and I spotted is no doubt being used to guide and communicate with a Cyber Fleet,' he told them.

Turner whistled. 'So that's what all those UFO things were . . . But there's been hundreds of sightings!' he breathed.

Isobel looked shocked. She turned to the Doctor anxiously. 'How do you think my uncle is involved in all this?' she asked.

'I don't know yet, my dear,' said the Doctor gently. He turned sharply to the Captain and asked him where the Brigadier was.

Turner told him. 'I'd better get onto him immediately at the MOD and give him your news,' he added breathlessly.

The Doctor held up a restraining hand. 'Wait a moment, Captain. I believe that your people discovered that visitors to Vaughn's headquarters seemed somehow different afterwards?'

'You think the Cybermen are controlling them?' suggested Zoe.

'Controlling them?' Turned echoed uneasily.

Zoe explained that the Cybermen were able to exert control over human minds but that the victims could appear to be almost normal.

'Who is the Brigadier immediately responsible to?' the Doctor inquired urgently.

'To Major-General Routledge, Doctor. He's with him now.'

The Doctor sprang to his feet as if galvanised into activity. 'Contact the Brigadier at once!' he cried. 'We must warn him!'

The Brigadier was pacing angrily round and round Routledge's dark and musty office, slapping his brown leather gloves against his leg, his eyes flashing with indignation.

'No cause for alarm!' he shouted scornfully. 'Billy, do you realise that they actually took potshots at a UNIT helicopter?'

Routledge leaned on his desk, smiling wryly. 'Alistair, your chaps were trespassing over their restricted area. What do you expect?'

'Oh, for heaven's sake, Billy, if Vaughn can't trust my mob then he must have a skeleton in the cupboard.'

The Major-General looked up sharply at this, his green eyes showing a momentary fear. 'I'm sorry. There is no action I can authorise,' he declared in an official tone.

Lethbridge-Stewart forced himself to calm down. 'Look, I know Vaughn's a powerful chap but there should at least be a discreet inquiry into his organisation,' he proposed reasonably.

Routledge started to blink rapidly. He mopped his forehead with a spotted handkerchief and cleared his throat awkwardly. 'It isn't our province,' he stalled, loosening his club tie and undoing his top shirt button.

'Then whose damned province is it?'

Routledge waved his hands about ineffectually. 'All you've given me is vague reports, Alistair. No conclusive evidence.'

This was too much for Lethbridge-Stewart. 'No evidence?' he shouted incredulously. 'What do you need, Billy? Corpses? Wreckage?' He stopped, noticing that a sickly pallor had crept over Routledge's face. 'What's the matter, Billy? Are you all right, old chap?' he asked with sincere concern.

Routledge dabbed at his glistening brow again. 'Course I am... It's nothing...' he mumbled. 'Probably all a terrible misunderstanding. Leave it with me, Alistair. I'll talk to the Home Office.'

The Brigadier waved his gloves dismissively. 'Talk's no good. I want immediate action, Billy.'

Routledge clutched at his temples and shook visibly. 'Impossible!' he shouted adamantly.

The Brigadier leaned across the desk, his eyes narrowing suspiciously. 'What sort of a hold has Vaughn got over you?' he murmured ominously.

For a few minutes Routledge remained silent, slumped awkwardly in his chair. Then he suddenly sprang up. 'Brigadier Lethbridge-Stewart, your forces will take no action whatsoever without my personal authorisation!' he hissed dangerously. 'That is an order.'

Taken aback by this abrupt transformation, the Brigadier stood to attention. 'General Routledge, you can override my authority but not that of UNIT Central Command, sir,' he declared through clenched teeth. 'I shall telex a full report to Field-Marshal Thatcher in Geneva and act according to his instructions. Good day, sir.'

With that, he turned smartly on his heel and strode out, jamming his cap firmly on his head.

Routledge sank shakily into his chair. After a while he touched a button on the videophone and the neat secretary appeared on the screen.

'Yes, General?'

With a supreme effort, Routledge pulled himself together. 'Get me International Electromatix Headquarters. Mr Vaughn. Top priority scramble...' he snapped, struggling to preserve his composure.

As Tobias Vaughn, closely followed by Packer, strode purposefully out of the private elevator into his London office, the videophone was bleeping urgently on the desk. At Vaughn's touch the screen flickered and the pale tense features of William Routledge appeared.

'This is priority scramble, Vaughn.'

'Yes, Routledge, what is it?' Vaughn demanded impatiently. 'I'm busy.'

'Listen, Vaughn, Lethbridge-Stewart's started stirring things up and I can't prevent him,' Routledge blurted out.

Vaughn snorted contemptuously. 'Nonsense, pull yourself together. You have the authority to...'

'I have no jurisdiction outside this country,' the General interrupted. 'He's sending a report to UNIT Command in Geneva. They're bound to investigate. I must say your staff were a bit heavy-handed.'

Vaughn threw a furious glance at Packer who was hovering at the window. 'Listen, Routledge, when will Geneva make a move against us?'

The General closed his eyes and pressed his fists against his temples. 'I think they... I think... they...' he stuttered feebly.

'What the hell's the matter with the man?' Packer snarled.

Vaughn ignored him, staring impassively at the videophone unit. 'Listen to me, Routledge...' he enunciated slowly. 'You will obey my instructions.'

Routledge shuddered and opened his eyes. 'Obey your instructions...' he repeated dutifully.

'You will leave your office immediately and come here to me.'

'Come to you...' The tortured face seemed to relax a little, but the eyes were pitifully confused.

'Do you understand, Routledge? You will tell no-one.'

'I understand. No-one. I obey. Now.'

The screen dazzled into static and went black.

Packer looked severely shaken. 'What's wrong with him?' he repeated nervously.

Vaughn frowned, clearly somewhat disturbed. 'Our control over him seems to be weakening,' he admitted.

'But that could be fatal,' Packer protested. 'If he doesn't obey you then we...'

Vaughn stood up, quickly regaining his customary bland manner. 'Oh, he will, Packer, he will,' he murmured confidently. Then he rounded sharply on his Deputy. 'What concerns me far more, Packer, is your bungling ineptitude. That is what has precipitated this whole crisis!'

Packer opened his mouth to object, but then closed it again and his resentment seeped away to collect like poisonous pus in a festering boil.

6
Secret Weapons

There was a tense hush in the Operations Room inside the Hercules while Captain Turner and Sergeant Walters tried to contact the Brigadier at the Ministry. To their dismay they learned that he had already left some time ago and that Major-General Routledge himself was no longer in the building.

'We're too late, Doctor, the Brig's already seen Routledge,' Turner reported despondently.

The Doctor shrugged. 'If I'm right and Routledge is under Vaughn's control the Brigadier will have had a wasted journey, I'm afraid.'

At that moment, Lethbridge-Stewart's voice surprised them. 'I loathe helicopters,' he boomed from the doorway. 'Utter waste of time, Doctor,' he announced, striding in and throwing his cap, baton and gloves onto his desk. 'The man's totally incompetent.'

The Doctor poured him a mug of strong tea from the vast pot, sat him down and quickly told him of his suspicions concerning Vaughn's real activities.

When he had finished, the Brigadier drank the sugarless tea in one prodigious gulp. 'This is incredible, Doctor,' he cried. 'Cybermen? Are you quite sure?'

'No more incredible than the Yeti,' smiled the Doctor.

'They seem to control some pretty important people,' Zoe remarked.

The Brigadier nodded. 'I wonder who else they have besides poor Billy Routledge. Doesn't give us much of a chance does it, Doctor?'

'Unless we can upset their plans before they invade,' the

Doctor speculated. 'But there are so many unknown factors . . .'

'Like where they're hiding all the Cybermen,' Jamie butted in.

'That's obvious,' Zoe told him. 'In Vaughn's London headquarters.'

'Not enough room,' Jamie objected. 'He's probably got an underground store or something.'

Zoe laughed mockingly. 'Oh, really, Jamie . . .'

The Doctor had been pouring himself some fresh tea. Suddenly he banged the heavy pot down. 'Jamie's quite right,' he exclaimed to everyone's surprise. 'Brigadier, would you by any chance have a map of the London sewerage system?'

At a resigned nod from his commander, Turner jumped up and soon returned with a large plastic sheet.

The Doctor eagerly swept aside the cluttered tray and examined the map. 'Aha!' he cried triumphantly. 'You see? There's a main flood relief channel running right underneath Vaughn's warehouse. Now, isn't that a coincidence!'

The Brigadier looked doubtful. 'What about the ah . . . the water down there: wouldn't that affect them?'

The Doctor shook his head. 'Anyway, such a tunnel would probably be mostly dry except after heavy rainfall,' he declared.

Isobel giggled. 'So what do we do? Pray for a cloudburst?'

The Brigadier glanced at her witheringly. 'Please, Miss Watkins, the future of the world may be at stake,' he scolded.

'I'm sorry, but it's just such a crazy idea to swallow,' she chuckled, nudging Zoe.

'So was the attack by the Yeti, miss. Nevertheless it happened.'

Captain Turner intervened tactfully. 'With respect, sir, she's right. If you go to Geneva with this story they'll think you've gone bananas.'

Lethbridge-Stewart sighed. 'Yes, Jimmy. We need some concrete evidence.'

The Doctor looked up from the map. 'What we need is some idea of the plan of attack,' he decided. 'Jamie, have you still got that ghastly little toy Mr Vaughn gave you?'

Jamie took the miniature radio from his waistcoat pocket and handed it over reluctantly. The Doctor opened the back and studied the monolithic circuitry again, muttering to himself in a strange technical jargon as he fiddled about. Eventually he turned to the Brigadier, his nostrils dilating as if he was beginning to pick up the scent of a fruitful investigation.

'Do you have any equipment here manufactured by International Electromatix?' he inquried eagerly.

'Indeed we do, Doctor. Mainframe computers, various radar and communications components . . .'

'Could I see them at once, please?'

The Brigadier nodded to Turner.

'This way, Doctor,' said the Captain, as the Doctor bounded out of his seat like a terrier. 'What exactly are you looking for?'

The Doctor grinned enigmatically. 'I don't know until I find it. A needle in a haystack perhaps!'

Major-General William Routledge sat hunched in the chair facing Tobias Vaughn across the gleaming curve of the desk, his expressionless eyes peering out from his bowed, lolling head. Packer hovered restlessly behind him.

'You must tell me,' Vaughn purred. 'How long before UNIT forces could act against me? How long?'

There was a brief silence. 'One . . . maybe two days . . .' Routledge said in a ghostly whisper.

Vaughn sat back with a smile of satisfaction. 'Time enough.'

Packer stepped forward. 'I don't like this. Suppose they move faster than that?'

'Let me do the supposing, Packer!' Vaughn snapped dangerously.

His Deputy stared down at their miserable, slumped victim whom his fingers were itching to torture and subdue. 'Yes, Mr Vaughn,' he whined submissively.

'There's a good fellow,' Vaughn smiled. 'Now, just to be on the safe side we'll conduct a little experiment. Have the Professor's Cerebration apparatus taken down to the warehouse. I'll join you there shortly.'

'What are you going to do?'

'Wait and see, Packer, wait and see.'

Packer poked Routledge as though he were a sack of potatoes. 'What about this?'

'Leave that to me. Now run along, Packer.'

Smarting under Vaughn's patronising treatment and frustrated in his desire to deal with Routledge, Packer slowly walked out.

Vaughn locked all the doors by remote control from his desk. Then he took out his fountain pen and twisted the top. The wall opposite the windows parted to reveal the glittering secret machine. As Vaughn walked over to the alcove, Routledge followed with his clouded eyes.

Vaughn gazed unblinking at the buzzing apparatus. 'There are some unexpected difficulties. We must therefore adjust the plan,' he informed it.

'Report the details. We will assess them,' rasped the metallic voice.

'We must bring the invasion forward.'

The machine crackled angrily. 'Our invasion force is not complete.'

'Nevertheless, the invasion must begin in thirteen terrestrial hours time,' Vaughn insisted unflinchingly. 'Otherwise we may face the combined forces of the entire world.'

Behind Vaughn, Routledge was now sitting upright, alert and listening.

'Your report is being assessed...' the machine announced, its central crystal revolving busily to and fro.

'You must accept my judgement or our partnership will terminate,' Vaughn threatened. 'The invasion will commence at dawn tomorrow.'

As Routledge stared at the bizarre and sinister apparatus in the alcove, his mind rapidly began to clear and a renewed glint of purpose gleamed in his eyes.

Vaughn stood his ground fearlessly while the Cyber Unit consulted with its masters. Eventually it replied in a dry brittle tone.

'It is agreed. Data will be revised and new schedules transmitted to you. Discussion terminated.'

With a victorious, preening toss of the head, Vaughn closed the shutters and turned round. He found himself staring down the barrel of a compact revolver.

'Dear me, Routledge . . .' he laughed after a momentary hesitation. 'Are you going to kill me?'

Routledge steadied himself on his feet and nodded. 'I must,' he croaked.

Slowly Vaughn walked towards him. 'But you can't kill me. I control you.'

Routledge backed away from him, holding the gun with both hands. 'I know what you've done to me,' he muttered, 'but I can fight it now.'

Vaughn continued his slow advance. 'No, you can't. And even if you could squeeze that trigger, you wouldn't be able to kill me,' he murmured almost hypnotically. 'Now turn the gun round and point it at your chest.'

Routledge uttered plaintive little whimpering noises as he watched his trembling hands turning the weapon round towards his own body. Tears of frustration ran down his cheeks as he fought to resist Vaughn's implacable will.

'Now, fire!'

Routledge's whole body shook with violent tremors, as if it were acting totally independently of his mind. Vaughn winced as a deafening crack split the air. Routledge remained standing like a waxen dummy for several seconds. Then he vomited a stream of blood and pitched forward onto his face at Vaughn's feet.

Shaking his head at the mess on the carpet, Vaughn strolled over to his desk and unlocked the doors.

Down in the warehouse, teams of technicians in protective suits were busy activating the lines of cocoons in their open containers, using portable machines identical to the one which the Doctor and Jamie had watched at work earlier.

Packer swaggered in and observed the process critically. 'Come on, get a move on!' he whined. 'Mr Vaughn's ordered a general shake-up down here.'

He watched the newest Cyberman glowing and bursting into life, a gasp of awe escaping from his bloodless lips as the monster emerged. It stood about two metres high, with a square head from which rightangled loops of hydraulic tubing protruded on either side. Its rudimentary face comprised two blank viewing lenses for eyes and a rectangular slit for a mouth. The broad chest contained a grilled ventilator unit which hissed nightmarishly. Thick flexible tubing ran along the arms and down each leg and was connected into a flattened humplike unit on the creature's back. Faint gasping and whirring noises inside the silvery body accompanied every movement. The movements were spasmodic and jerky at first, but gradually they grew suppler and more human as the creature strode across to take its place among the assembled ranks of activated Cybermen standing motionless and silent in row upon row in the centre of the warehouse.

With a shiver of excitement, Packer marched across to a large steel panel in the brick end-wall of the building. Opening it with a special key, he threw several switches in the control box behind the panel. A section of the warehouse wall began to rotate, slowly revealing a bare brick chamber about a metre above the floor level of the warehouse. In the centre of the chamber was a circular well about two metres in diameter, covered by a domed steel lid hinged at one side. A short flight of steps led up to the chamber level and a steel railing ran round the well at hip-height.

Packer threw more switches and with a grinding hum the massive lid gradually opened up into the vertical position, locking itself with a series of echoing clunks. Packer closed the panel and locked it. Then he walked over and climbed onto the raised platform, staring down into the fetid darkness. Stout steel ladders clamped to the mouldering brickwork led down from the rim of the well into a huge shaft. Eerie sounds echoed up from the darkness and a cold, dank breeze wafted fitfully into his face. Like an admiral on his poop deck, Packer grasped the handrail and turned to the ranks of motionless Cybermen.

'First Legion,' he snapped. A dozen Cybermen hissed into life and lumbered heavily forward. 'You have your instructions?' Packer demanded.

'Affirmative,' chorused the creatures with an exhalation of rubbery breath.

'Phase one. Proceed through tunnels to your allotted sector and stand by for Phase Two,' Packer ordered, thoroughly enjoying his newfound powers.

The Cybermen jerked forward and marched with creaking, hissing determination up the steps and onto the platform. Then, one by one, they swung themselves onto the ladders and down into the shaft. Steadying himself on the handrail, Packer grinned with delight as he watched the disciplined, obedient monsters disappearing underground, trying not to retch at the sickly, oily exhalations they released as they passed him.

'Second Legion. Proceed,' he commanded, swelling with self-importance.

At that moment, Vaughn hurried out of the nearby elevator followed by Mr Gregory who was struggling with the delicate but heavy mechanism of the Cerebration Mentor in his scrawny arms. Vaughn paused for a moment out of sight, watching Packer's antics with scornful amusement. Then he strode forward.

'There you are, Packer. Everything going according to plan?'

'Yes Mr Vaughn,' Packer preened himself.

'Excellent. Time for our little experiment.'

Gregory set down the Professor's machine on the steps. 'Mr Vaughn, sir, I don't think this is wise,' he ventured timidly.

Vaughn rounded on him. 'It would be even more unwise not to test,' he hissed under his breath. 'We must be sure that we have an effective weapon against the Cybermen.'

Packer looked alarmed. 'You actually intend to use that thing?'

Ignoring him, Vaughn strode across to the nearest cocoon awaiting regeneration. 'I am a man of science, Packer, not a cowardly sadist,' he snapped, motioning to two technicians to connect the portable bioprojector to the cocoon. 'Now, partially activate. Just sufficiently to enable it to emerge,' he instructed.

The technicians started up the process. Within a few seconds the Cyberman came to life amid a shower of sparks and fibres and the piercing undulating whine. As soon as it had broken free they switched off and the monster froze, halfway out of its container. Vaughn nodded his approval and gestured to Gregory to prepare the Cerebration device.

'Connect up Watkins's little box of tricks,' he said impatiently.

Reluctantly Gregory plugged two leads into the machine and then fitted the pads, to which they were connected, on either side of the creature's head.

Vaughn took a step or two back as a precaution. 'I'm waiting,' he prompted.

Gregory's hands hovered hesitantly over the controls. 'Please, Mr Vaughn, we don't know what effect this is going to have ...' he pleaded.

Vaughn cast his eyes to the roof in despair. 'Exactly. That is precisely why we are conducting this experiment,' he explained painstakingly. 'Now get on with it, Gregory.'

'What er ... what emotion shall I attempt to induce?' Gregory mumbled.

Vaughn considered for a moment. 'Fear, I think. Let's see how our mighty ally reacts to fear,' he suggested eagerly.

Gregory selected settings and pressed buttons and then retreated like a child lighting a firework.

There was a faint clicking sound and the Cyberman twitched slightly.

'Increase power,' Vaughn shouted, his good eye narrowing like the other as he observed the effect intently.

The clicks increased in frequency. The Cyberman

started to writhe and clutched at the pads convulsively.

'More power!' Vaughn yelled.

'Now it's at maximum . . .' Gregory shouted, adjusting the settings and taking refuge behind the nearest stack of containers.

The clicks ran together into a strident pinging sound. Uttering grating, guttural cries of distress the Cyberman tore off the pads and wheeled about, flailing the air with its powerful arms. Packer whipped out his pistol and emptied the magazine into the Cyberman's chest, but the shots had no effect and he was sent reeling across the warehouse by a vicious blow from the monster's fist.

'I warned you. The device isn't tuned yet . . .' Gregory screamed.

The crazed Cyberman suddenly turned and staggered up the steps into the chamber over the sewer shaft, shrieking like knife blades scraping against each other.

'It's following the others into the sewers!' Packer gasped, hauling himself to his feet in a daze.

'Let it go,' Vaughn ordered impassively, still standing his ground as the Cyberman disappeared into the echoing shaft.

'The thing's gone berserk. It could've killed me!' Packer blustered, reloading his pistol as he walked unsteadily over to Vaughn.

The Director smiled sourly. 'Yes, I think we have established that Watkins's device can be effective. Get him back to work on it immediately, Gregory. I want more power and remote directional control,' he declared.

The cringing Research Director nodded meekly and set about disconnecting the lethal machine.

'But what about that Cyberman? We can't leave it rampaging about down there,' Packer protested. 'It'll destroy everything in its path.'

'Excellent,' Vaughn purred. 'Anyone foolish enough to be down there deserves to die.'

With a nod to the awed technicians, Vaughn turned and strode back to his elevator.

The Brigadier was getting rather irritated with the incessant chatter between Zoe, Isobel and Jamie which was disturbing his concentration while he tried to draft his report for Central Command in Geneva.

'If you believe those Cyber things are in the sewers why not go down and get some proof?' Isobel suggested for the umpteenth time.

The Brigadier threw down his pen in exasperation. 'And how do I prove that in the London sewers there lurks an army of robots from outer space poised to invade us?' he scoffed. 'Go and capture one?'

'No need,' Isobel retorted cheerfully. 'Just get some photographs.'

The Brigadier considered her for a moment, his annoyance changing to mild interest. 'Not a bad idea, miss,' he admitted, 'but it's pitch dark down there.'

Isobel shrugged this off casually. 'Okay, so you use an infra-red film with a number 25 filter and telephoto lens. It'd be a cinch.'

The Brigadier frowned. 'Is that gibberish, or do you know what you're talking about, miss?'

'Course I do!' said Isobel indignantly. 'All I need is my camera from Uncle's friend's house.'

The Brigadier grunted. 'Oh no, my dear, this would be a job for our lads.'

'Of all the cretinous bigoted chauvinists . . .' spluttered Isobel, turning to Zoe for support.

'I'll get in touch with our photoreconnaissance unit . . .' declared the Brigadier, marching briskly away.

Isobel grimaced after him. 'Oh you . . . you *man*!' she shouted.

'Och, he's right,' Jamie muttered.

Zoe stared at the grinning young Scot in sheer disgust. 'Jamie McCrimmon, just because you're a man . . . well, a boy anyway, you think you're superior.'

Jamie raised his eyebrows innocently. 'I didn'a say that . . . but it's true!'

Zoe nudged Isobel in sisterly solidarity. 'Righto. Come on,' she cried.

Isobel looked nonplussed for a moment, then the penny

dropped. She linked arms with Zoe. 'What a splendid idea,' she agreed and they moved towards the door at the rear of the Operations Room.

Jamie barred their way. 'Hey, now where do ye wee lassies think ye're going?' he demanded.

'Should we let him come?' Zoe consulted her new ally.

Isobel grinned. 'Well, men aren't usually much good in such dangerous situations,' she objected.

Jamie persisted. 'What are ye up to?'

'We're off to London to take some photographs,' said Zoe. 'Coming?'

Jamie looked shocked. 'London? Listen lassie, ye shouldn't go anywhere without telling the Doctor.'

Zoe stuck out her chin with characteristic defiance. 'Okay, Goody Goody. You tell him.'

She and Isobel pushed Jamie aside and marched out to find the friendly Transport Corporal and persuade him to arrange a secret lift for them.

Jamie hesitated, unsure whether to say anything to the Doctor. 'Och, here we go again...' he muttered at last, trailing uncertainly after the rebellious females, determined not to be left out...

Captain Turner crept back into the Operations Computer Room to find the Doctor still engrossed in a piece of circuitry he had removed from the mainframe cabinet of the Hercules's central processor. With a non-committal sigh the Doctor let the watchmaker's eyeglass drop into his lap.

'Found something?' Turner asked quietly.

'Yes!' cried the Doctor confidently. 'And no,' he added, holding up the circuit from the International Electromatix computer and the small back panel from Jamie's transistor. 'These two micromonolithic systems seem to match...'

'What do they do?'

The Doctor shook his head with a baffled frown. 'I don't know, young man, but I do know that they have no useful function in either your central processor or in Jamie's wireless.'

Turner waited, hoping for some enlightenment, but the Doctor brooded silently over the mysterious panels.

'Why put in a circuit that has no function?' Turner muttered.

The Doctor stood up, weighing the components thoughtfully in his hands. 'Oh, they serve a function all right, Captain. I'm convinced that these monolithic systems have something to do with the Cybermen. But I need to conduct certain tests . . .'

'I'm sure we can arrange whatever facilities you require,' Turner offered promptly.

The Doctor thanked him politely. 'However I think I'll find what I need among Professor Watkins's equipment in Professor Travers's basement in London if you don't mind,' he said.

They went through into the Operations Room, where the Brigadier had just finished briefing his photo-reconnaissance unit over the radiotelephone.

The Doctor looked around for his three young associates. 'Where are Jamie and Zoe and Isobel . . .?' he asked in some alarm.

'No idea,' shrugged the Brigadier, busy at his desk.

'Excuse me sir,' piped up Sergeant Walters, 'but Corporal Benton's driven them into London.'

'Benton's what!' exploded Lethbridge-Stewart.

'Said they had to get some vital evidence for you, sir.'

The Brigadier looked appalled. 'Evidence for me? Get Benton on the R/T immediately,' he shouted.

The Doctor looked up from the circuits, utterly bewildered. 'What on earth is going on?' he asked plaintively.

The Brigadier took the Doctor aside. 'I'm sorry, Doctor, but while my back was turned those crazy kids got it into their heads to slip back to London to try to obtain photographs of Cybermen . . . no doubt from the sewers.'

The Doctor flapped his arms aimlessly. 'Oh, my goodness me!' he gasped, completely at a loss.

The Brigadier fumed silently while he waited for Benton to make contact. 'Benton? At last. What the devil's going on?' he yelled into the radiotelephone.

'Sorry, sir, I thought it was official. The young ladies told me you'd authorised them to fetch some important photographs from town so I...'

'So you succumbed to the charms of the fair sex... as usual,' the Brigadier shouted acidly. 'Where are they now?'

'I've just dropped them in the vicinity of Blue Sector One, sir... corner of Chaplin Street.'

'That's close to Vaughn's headquarters, sir,' Walters put in smartly, listening on the extension.

'Get them back at once!' ordered Lethbridge-Stewart.

'I'll try, sir, but I'm not sure which way they've gone...' crackled Benton sheepishly.

'Then find out, Benton, find out. Otherwise you're in deep trouble,' the Brigadier threatened, purple cheeked with rage. He slammed the receiver down and seized Turner's arm. 'You'd better take a small force to the area, Jimmy, just in case.'

Turner saluted and hurried out.

The Doctor pulled himself together. 'I'd better go back to London with him. I want to do some tests on these circuits,' he informed the Brigadier. 'They may be connected with the Cybermen. I'll leave my three young friends in your capable hands, Brigadier...' And he shuffled out after the Captain.

'Don't worry, Doctor, we'll find them,' Lethbridge-Stewart promised. But his face was furrowed with anxious foreboding as he watched the Doctor depart.

7

Underground Operations

The eerily flickering pinpoints of light in the crystal cast a macabre pattern over Vaughn's and Packer's faces as they listened to the Cyber Unit rasping in its alcove.

'One hour before Invasion the Cyber transmitter units will be launched into Earth orbit. Transmission will penetrate to all areas with immediate effect...' it croaked with sinister detachment.

'And if it doesn't work?' Vaughn inquired calmly.

The Cyber Unit sparked menacingly. 'Humans cannot resist Cyber control. Cyber forces will select suitable humans for conversion. Unsuitable humans will be eliminated,' it announced.

Packer glanced anxiously at Vaughn. 'Conversion into Cybermen?' he breathed.

'Affirmative.'

Vaughn's face betrayed a hint of vulnerability. 'This is not as we agreed,' he murmured.

'It has been decided,' rasped the machine.

'No!' rapped Vaughn. 'We agreed that I should remain in control of the Earth and supply the minerals you require. You will honour our agreement, otherwise there will be no invasion.' His pale eyes were filled with a wild fire.

The Cyber Unit oscillated with ominous precision. 'To retain such control you must complete your conversion, Vaughn. You must become one of us.'

Vaughn shook his head vehemently. 'No. My body may be cybernetic but my mind will remain human,' he vowed.

Packer trembled in the shadows as the machine stopped

flickering and there was a long, tense silence. Vaughn waited, outwardly calm but inwardly strung like a piano wire.

Eventually the Cyber Unit sparked into life again. 'It has been agreed. Discussion terminated,' it croaked, falling silent and still.

Vaughn twisted the pen cap in his pocket and the alcove closed up again.

'You're taking a terrible, terrible risk opposing them,' Packer whispered shakily.

Vaughn chuckled drily. 'My dear Packer, they need me. I know they'll try to take control away from me once the invasion is completed, but they don't know about the Cerebration Machine, do they? That's our trump card.'

Packer looked scared and sceptical. 'How do we know the Cyber transmissions won't affect us as well?' he challenged.

Vaughn smiled complacently, his silver hair shining in the fading light. 'We shall be protected by the implanted shielding capsules,' he reminded him, tapping the back of his neck. 'You see I've thought of everything, Packer. Everything.'

In the deserted back street, Jamie heaved at the heavy manhole cover while Zoe and Isobel, with her photographic gear slung around her neck, looked on admiringly. At last the iron cover shifted and swung open with a tremendous clang. Mopping his glistening face, Jamie knelt and peered into the gloom.

'Third time lucky,' he gasped thankfully.

'Okay, down you go,' Zoe prompted.

Jamie hesitated. 'Och, at least let's contact the Doctor first,' he pleaded.

'Scared, Jamie?' Zoe twinkled.

He glared at her. 'All right, lassie, just you wait,' he muttered, lowering himself into the manhole and clambering down the rusty metal ladder set into the shaft.

Zoe winked at Isobel and followed him down.

Just as Isobel followed suit, she heard a shout in the

distance. A young policeman was striding rapidly along the street towards them.

'It's the fuzz!' she warned, scrambling onto the ladder and disappearing into the sewer.

The constable broke into a run, shouting to her to stop. Reaching the manhole he called into the dank darkness after them: 'What are you doing down there, you young idiots? Come on out or I'll be down there after you!'

At the bottom of the deep shaft the intrepid trio huddled together listening helplessly as the policeman's threats echoed down the tunnels.

'If he goes on like this we'll have every Cyberman in the area on top of us...' moaned Jamie.

'If there are any,' Isobel giggled nervously.

Zoe grasped each of them by the arm. 'I think there's something along that tunnel,' she warned.

Isobel opened her camera case and fiddled with the telephoto lens attachment. 'I can't see anything... but just in case . . .' she murmured bravely.

Jamie peered in the direction Zoe had indicated. 'I think perhaps we should get out of here,' he advised in a quavering voice.

But Zoe led them both determinedly forward into the damp darkness. 'This is what we came for,' she reminded them.

They soon reached a junction. Zoe chose a branch of the fork and cautiously crept forward with the other two trailing timidly behind her. Suddenly Zoe stopped. 'Yes, I was right,' she whispered. 'Look there.'

They strained to see along the oval, brick-lined sewer with just a trickle of water in the bottom. A vague shape was just discernible by another junction.

'You kids come on out,' called the constable from the shaft. 'Stop mucking around.'

'Och, ah wish he'd shut up,' Jamie grunted, clenching his teeth to stop them chattering.

There was a chilling silence. The dim shape stirred. Hissing and high-pitched bubbling sounds echoed along the tunnel as the Cyberman turned and started lumbering towards them.

'Fantastic!' gasped Isobel, adjusting the settings and hastily clicking the shutter button.

Jamie clutched Zoe's cold hand. 'Come on, let's get out.'

But Zoe seemed rooted to the spot, staring at the lurching silver figure as its warm, acrid breath wafted past them.

'Wait,' Isobel begged. 'I must get a close up... This is absolutely marvellous.'

'Where are you?' yelled the policeman from somewhere behind them.

Isobel's shutter whirred incessantly. She seemed fearless and utterly fascinated by the advancing apparition.

Jamie could stand it no longer. He grabbed the girls by the hand and started dragging them back to the shaft. 'Will ye come away? Ye don't know what yon things can do to a body,' he muttered at Isobel.

Every few steps, Isobel turned and shot a few more frames of the huge creature creaking and hissing behind them.

'What's that...Who... who are you...?' they heard the policeman yelling ahead of them.

Next moment two vivid flashes of light sizzled in the distance. A dreadful scream tore into their ears and froze them to the spot.

'The... policeman...' gasped Isobel in the awful silence.

'Cybermen must have killed him,' Zoe muttered.

'Killed him?' Isobel quavered, as if suddenly it was no longer all a kind of game.

The grating and rasping sounds were coming at them from both directions now. Jamie whipped round. The pursuing Cyberman was staggering drunkenly towards them.

'We're trapped,' he gasped. 'They've got us.'

'What can we do?' Isobel screamed, breaking into a hysterical shaking.

Jamie pushed the girls into the other arm of the junction they had reached and shielded them with his body as the Cyberman began screeching and wildly flailing as if striking at an invisible foe. He closed his eyes and waited for the searing blast from the monster's laser units. But the maddened Cyberman lurched past them as if they were not there and disappeared in the direction of the shaft.

They gazed after it in amazement.

'It ignored us...' murmured Zoe, trembling with relief.

'Aye,' Jamie gulped. 'It looked almost mad.'

'It was frightened,' said Isobel, calming down, 'just like us...'

Corporal Benton stood indecisively beside his jeep staring into the open manhole, his stomach turning at the smell of burnt human flesh rising from the shaft and his ears ringing with the policeman's dying screams. A second jeep carrying Captain Turner, a sergeant and two privates rounded the corner and squealed to a halt next to him. Benton gave Turner a brief report and Turner immediately led his squad cautiously down the rickety metal rungs into the shaft.

They averted their faces as Turner's flashlight picked out the young constable's scorched remains a few metres along the tunnel. The gaping terror-stricken face was puckered like shrivelled polythene.

Turner called out softly at first, then more loudly: 'McCrimmon... Zoe... Miss Watkins... Can you hear me? This is Captain Turner.'

The flashlight beam showed the empty tunnel curving gradually into the distance. There was no response.

'Reckon they've copped it as well, sir?' asked the sergeant quietly.

Turner began to advance slowly. 'These tunnels are a maze. They could be anywhere...' he whispered. Then he stopped abruptly. 'I think there's someone up ahead.'

Next moment the five men uttered a chorus of astonished gasps as two silver figures stalked into view round the curve.

'Blimey... what the 'ell are they?' exclaimed the sergeant as five safety catches snapped off in unison.

'Hold your fire!' Turner ordered calmly. 'Move back

slowly. I think we've found our evidence.'

Isobel tried to wrench free from Jamie's restraining grasp. 'But it's my dolly soldier,' she insisted. 'At least let's tell him we're here.'

Jamie was adamant. 'Wait, there are Cybermen between us. We daren't give ourselves away.'

'The next lot might not be so shortsighted,' Zoe pointed out wryly.

They listened. The Cybermen's terrible tramping seemed to recede in the direction of Turner's voice.

'I do hope James is not alone . . .' Isobel murmured with a shiver.

The squad backed away from the looming aliens as they advanced, hissing and whirring menacingly.

'Grenades, Sergeant . . .' Turner whispered.

The sergeant unhitched three grenades from his belt and carefully handed them round.

'Do not resist!' one of the Cybermen suddenly warned in a grating voice. 'You will obey instructions.'

'What must we do?' Turner answered steadily, gesticulating behind his back.

'Pins out,' whispered the sergeant. 'Ready, sir.'

'You will come with us. Obey or we shall destroy you.'

All at once the two Cybermen swung round as the guttural cries of the berserk third Cyberman suddenly erupted behind them.

'Now!' Turner breathed.

The sergeant and the privates hurled the primed grenades down the tunnel and the squad threw themselves face down on the slimy brick floor. The grenades rolled among the feet of the Cybermen as two of them grappled with the crazed newcomer. Three explosions followed in rapid succession and the sewer filled with smoke and flying fragments.

As the smoke cleared, the incredulous soldiers saw the crazed alien lurching to its feet. It seemed indestructible as it jerked inexorably towards them, screeching metallically.

'Get it, Perkins!' yelled the sergeant.

Private Perkins fumbled desperately with the pin of a fourth grenade. Just as he yanked it out, the Cyberman's laser unit strobed with a blinding blue light. Perkins threw up his arms and staggered backwards, his uniform ablaze and his frozen face a treacly mask. The primed grenade clattered along the tunnel towards the crouching squad. Diving forward, Turner seized it and flung it back at the advancing Cyberman. The grenade exploded in the monster's chest unit and thick black fluid pumped copiously out of the severed tubes as part of the tunnel roof collapsed onto its head.

While the sergeant attended to Perkins, Captain Turner cautiously approached the three prone aliens half-buried under the smoking rubble. He could still hear the faint sound of strangled mechanical breathing. He shouted urgently into the darkness.

'Jamie . . . Zoe . . . Isobel . . . If you can hear me come out quickly . . .'

To his relief he heard a faint cry of acknowledgement from Isobel. 'There's not much time,' he yelled. 'Quick as you can this way!'

'Perkins is dead, sir,' reported the sergeant. 'Harris copped a shrapnel splinter in the shoulder.'

'Right, get him out of here,' Turner ordered, covering the still breathing Cybermen with his machine pistol while Benton and the sergeant manhandled Harris to the manhole shaft.

'Get a move on, you idiots . . .' Turner shouted, peering into the tunnel as one of the Cybermen's hands started twitching spasmodically.

Eventually he heard running footsteps and the three fugitives suddenly appeared round the curve shouting excitedly.

'James . . . thank goodness you're . . .'

'Shut up and get out of here,' Turner snapped, jerking his head towards the shaft.

Isobel scowled. 'Well, there's no need to be so rude!' she retorted.

'I've already lost one good man because of you lot and I don't want to lose any more,' Turner said, bundling them roughly past the gasping Cybermen and the hideous corpse of Private Perkins.

'See any more behind you?' he asked Jamie as the girls clambered up the ladder.

'No,' Jamie mumbled shamefacedly.

'Well, give me a hand with Perkins's body,' Turner snapped, 'And watch out. Those Cyber things are still breathing.'

Jamie helped sling the corpse over Turner's shoulder and started to follow him painfully slowly up the ladder to the street.

Suddenly there was a croaking roar from below. Jamie looked down and saw the glinting figure of one of the Cybermen shaking itself free from the rubble and lumbering towards the shaft. Above him, Turner was just struggling out of the manhole helped by Benton and the sergeant. Jamie scrambled up the ladder for dear life, but just as he reached the surface his ankle was seized in a crushing grip. Screaming with pain and panic, he fought to free his foot. Benton and Turner each took an arm and tried to drag him clear, while the sergeant knelt down and smashed the Cyberman again and again on the head with a rifle butt.

At last the weakened Cyberman released its grip and Jamie was hauled out. Then the sergeant dropped a grenade into the Cyberman's arms and he and Benton heaved the heavy iron manhole cover back into place. The thick plate shook as a muffled explosion spurted smoke round its edges. They all watched the manhole cover in the ensuing silence. It did not stir.

'I don't believe it,' gasped the sergeant. 'Them things are almost indestructible.'

Turner glanced over at the jeep where Zoe and Isobel were making Private Harris comfortable. 'Maybe, but we're not,' he snapped, helping Jamie to hobble. 'Let's get out of here.'

As the Doctor poked among the monolithic circuitry with

two probes, frowning unhappily at the wavering traces on the oscilloscope beside him, he didn't notice the Brigadier quietly enter the makeshift laboratory in the basement of Professor Travers's London house.

'Any success, Doctor?'

'Ah, Brigadier. Not yet I fear. There's an alien logic in these circuits, but I haven't managed to work it out yet,' smiled the Doctor, rubbing his tired eyes.

Lethbridge-Stewart yawned. 'The Watkins girl's just developing her snapshots upstairs. I'm taking a full report to Geneva in the morning.'

'How long will that take?'

'Depends. Should get some action in a day or two.'

The Doctor stared dubiously at the oscilloscope screen. 'That could be too late,' he warned glumly.

Just then Isobel burst in waving some large photographic prints still dripping wet. Zoe and Jamie followed.

'There you are, Brig! Aren't they beauties?' Isobel cried, laying the black and white prints out on the bench.

The Brigadier glanced at the greyish, blurred shapes unenthusiastically. 'Er . . . Well done, Miss Watkins . . .' he muttered, turning back to the Doctor.

'What's wrong with them?' Isobel demanded in a wounded tone.

The Brigadier attempted a conciliatory smile. 'I don't want to hurt your professional pride, Miss Watkins, but to be honest they look a little like . . . well, fakes.'

'But they're Cybermen,' Jamie protested. 'Anyone can see that, ye Sassenach!'

The Brigadier smiled condescendingly. '*You* can because you've seen them before. But *I* have to convince a bunch of sceptical international defence experts.'

All at once the Doctor leaped up like a Jack-in-the-box. 'Yes, of course . . .' he cried.

'What?' Zoe asked eagerly.

But the Doctor sat down again just as abruptly, resuming his tinkering without another word.

Vaughn and Packer stood in the subdued light of the

suspended spherical lamps, looking out at the lights of the city under the darkening sky.

'It was definitely a UNIT force. They destroyed two Cybermen,' reported Packer despondently.

'How clever of them,' purred Vaughn.

'But they got out alive, sir. The authorities will know by now,' Packer whined.

Vaughn shrugged disinterestedly. 'They are powerless to stop us. In a few hours the invasion will be completed. We shall control all that...' he murmured, gesturing expansively through the window.

A buzzer sounded.

'That will be Gregory. The Professor's machine must be ready, sir.'

'Excellent. Let them in, Packer.'

Gregory entered, followed by Professor Watkins carrying his Cerebration Mentor like a precious baby. It looked lighter and more compact and the earphone pads had been replaced by a long, narrowly tapering horn.

'We've added narrow bandwidth transducers to focus the output directionally,' Gregory announced, as the Professor placed the device on Vaughn's desk and turned his back on it.

'This is sheer madness,' Watkins shouted. 'That machine is now a deadly weapon.'

'I compliment your efficiency,' Vaughn murmured, examining the device approvingly.

'Those modifications were totally unnecessary,' Watkins protested, blinking unhappily behind his thick glasses.

'For your purposes perhaps, Professor. But I have a somewhat different use for your little gadget.'

Watkins rounded on his tormentor. 'Do what you will. It's yours. Now just give me my niece and let us go free.'

Vaughn laughed urbanely. 'My dear fellow, your niece is already at liberty and no doubt sitting comfortably at home.' He turned to his Chief Researcher. 'Now Gregory, how does one operate this thing?'

'Isobel free? I don't believe you!' Watkins whimpered, realising his utter helplessness now.

'Careful, Mr Vaughn,' Gregory warned, as Vaughn

picked up the device and pointed it at Watkins.

'Dangerous is it?' Vaughn sneered, pressing a sequence of switches.

Watkins backed away, wide-eyed with terror. 'Don't... don't point it...' he beseeched him.

'Do you know what fear is?' Vaughn taunted as the machine began emitting its evil clicking sounds, rising rapidly to a piercing whistle.

Watkins shut his eyes and pressed his hands over his ears, moaning pitifully.

'Mr Vaughn, you could kill him!' Gregory warned, trying to intervene. Packer held him back, watching the torture with excited eyes.

'We must make sure he's done his work thoroughly,' Vaughn laughed, increasing the power so that the whistling rose even higher.

Watkins's glasses fell off his nose as he writhed and cowered against the wall, his kindly eyes popping widely open as he focussed on some imaginary horror. He started punching wildly at the air as if warding off some loathsome attacker and then uttered strangled squeaks of submission. Impassively Vaughn watched the cringing old man slide down the wall to his knees, sobbing with fear. Then he switched off the machine and put it back on the desk.

'Most effective,' he beamed. 'I congratulate you, Professor. Such a pity we cannot test it at full strength. However, we have further need of your expertise.'

Watkins peered blindly up at him, foaming at the lips and trembling with shock.

Vaughn turned to Gregory. 'You will take the Professor back to the complex immediately. I want these devices on the production lines at once.'

Packer yanked the old man to his feet and shoved his glasses back onto his nose.

'You force me to work for you, Vaughn,' Watkins suddenly burst out in a hoarse whisper. 'You are an evil man. I pity you, but given the chance I shall kill you.'

Vaughn gazed at the hunched figure, momentarily disconcerted by his victim's impassioned threat. 'Kill me, Professor?' he mocked. 'Would you really?'

Watkins nodded vigorously.

Vaughn walked over and took Packer's machine pistol out of its holster. He thrust it into Watkins's hand. 'What are you waiting for?' he laughed, slapping the old man's tear-stained cheek. 'Shoot me!'

Watkins stared at the gun, then at Vaughn in bewilderment.

'Shoot me!' Vaughn shouted, sending Watkins reeling with another vicious slap before walking away a few paces and turning.

Recovering his balance, the Professor fired a burst. Shots smashed into lamps and a video screen.

Vaughn shook his head derisively. 'Surely you can do better than that?' he taunted. 'Try again.'

Racked with conflicting emotions, Watkins hesitated. Then he took careful aim and fired again. Several holes appeared in Vaughn's jacket and shirt as bullets ricochetted round the office. Vaughn threw back his head and laughed at Watkins's incredulous stare.

'Take him away and get the device into production!' he cried, casually flicking the torn shreds of cloth off his jacket.

In Travers's basement the Doctor was still struggling to solve the riddle of the monolithic circuitry. Jamie was fast asleep in an old armchair with his injured foot propped on a cushion, while Jimmy Turner sat sleepily by his portable radiotelephone unit on the workbench.

Isobel brought in some tea and shortcake biscuits and sat down beside him. 'Am I forgiven?' she asked.

Turner grinned. 'Not really your fault, I suppose,' he murmured, patting her hand.

'I just didn't realise about the Cybermen...' Isobel explained. 'I've been listening to Zoe telling the Brigadier all about them for his report.'

Turner shook his head in amazement. 'We hit 'em with four or five grenades and one still survived! I'd hate to have to tackle a whole army of the things.'

Suddenly the Doctor threw down the circuits in despair. 'No, no, no,' he muttered, rubbing his bleary eyes irritably as he rose and walked about restlessly.

'What's the matter?' Jamie gasped, waking with a start and wincing at the pain in his ankle.

The Doctor ignored him, absently picking up Turner's tea and sipping it deep in thought again.

At that moment the radiotelephone bleeped. Turner answered it, asking Isobel to fetch the Brigadier.

'What's the flap?' asked Lethbridge-Stewart, taking the receiver.

'Benton reported from Blue Sector One, sir,' Sergeant Walters's voice informed him mushily. 'At 2130 hours he saw two security guards and another man leaving the IE Headquarters with Professor Watkins. He's on their tail now.'

'We could intercept and release the Professor, sir,' suggested Turner listening on the extension.

Isobel looked anxiously at the Brigadier.

He frowned. 'I don't like the idea, Jimmy,' he said after a pause.

'Oh come on! Please!' Isobel begged him, clutching his sleeve.

The Doctor cleared his throat noisily. 'Brigadier, the Professor might be able to help me solve this problem,' he said, waving the two monolithic circuits.

The Brigadier looked unhappy at the risk of further trouble before his mission to UNIT Command in Geneva.

'It could be a vital chance for a breakthrough,' the Doctor urged him.

Lethbridge-Stewart considered the two earnest faces. Finally he relented. 'All right. It's your show, Jimmy, but be careful,' he said reluctantly.

Isobel hugged him and gave him a smacking kiss on the cheek.

'Tell Benton to stay with them. I'll contact him en route. I'm on my way, Sergeant,' rapped Turner into the receiver.

'Vaughn's lot know we mean business now,' the Brigadier warned him. 'They won't be playing games.'

'Neither will I, sir!' Turner promised and he dashed out with Isobel staring admiringly after him.

The Brigadier, still blushing from the kiss, reached

across and handed the plate to Isobel. 'Care for a biscuit?' he asked gallantly.

An owl hooted somewhere in the nearby trees. Turner and three UNIT soldiers sat tensely in their jeep at the deserted crossroads, listening to Benton's regular reports on the radio giving the position of the International Electromatix company car carrying Gregory and Professor Watkins back to the factory complex. Thin trails of cloud scudded across the Moon, giving it a covert, lurking appearance high above them.

'About a kilometre from your position now, sir,' Benton suddenly blurted.

'Go!' snapped Turner to his driver. The jeep swept out of the side lane and drew across the narrow road, completely blocking it. The driver cut the engine and the lights and the four men whipped out their pistols and jumped into the surrounding hedgerows.

Twenty seconds later, a set of powerful headlights sliced the darkness, followed by another, some distance behind but gaining rapidly. The International Electromatix car screamed to a halt a few metres from the jeep. As one of Vaughn's men got out to investigate, the UNIT force emerged with levelled pistols and challenged him. The man yelled something and the limousine started reversing, but Benton's Jaguar roared up behind and cut off its retreat. Another man jumped out and they both opened fire on Turner's squad. While the UNIT squad fired back, Professor Watkins opened the rear door of the limousine and scuttled towards the undergrowth along the lane. Gregory leaped out after him and raised a revolver at his back. Before he could shoot the Professor, Benton fired from his car and Gregory fell dead on the grass verge. At the same instant, Turner's advancing force killed one of the Professor's escort and the other one fled into the woods and got away.

Turner ushered the shocked and dazed Professor gently into the Jaguar and he and Benton drove him swiftly back to London with the rest of the squad escorting them in the jeep.

In Vaughn's darkened office Packer was smacking his bony fists together with impotent rage.

'It was a UNIT group again,' he fumed, his mean eyes glittering malevolently at his master. 'I warned you, but you ignored me.'

'Still sceptical, Packer?' Vaughn inquired calmly, reclining in his chair with his eyes closed.

'Well, what can we do now?' Packer whined. 'We've only got one machine. Now they've got Watkins back and Gregory's dead we can't manufacture any more, can we?'

If Tobias Vaughn was at all worried by the recent kidnapping he betrayed no sign of disquiet. 'Once Cyber Control is transmitting the coercion signal the Doctor and his friends will be utterly helpless,' he reminded Packer. 'You'll be able to pick them up and enjoy your revenge. Can I trust you to accomplish that?'

Packer stared at Vaughn's shadowy figure with gnawing hatred. 'Of course!' he snapped petulantly.

'Good.' Vaughn glanced at his luminous digital watch. 'Now, I suggest that you get some rest,' he murmured. 'There remain just five and one half hours until the invasion begins . . .'

8

Invasion

Professor Watkins gratefully drank several cups of tea, clutching his niece's hand with affectionate relief. Then he nibbled at a biscuit and gazed in bewilderment at the ring of faces around him.

'I know nothing,' he admitted regretfully, 'nothing at all.'

The Doctor sighed dejectedly. 'You've no idea what these micromonolithic circuits are for, Professor?' he asked for the third or fourth time.

'I'm sorry, Doctor,' Watkins smiled feebly. 'I don't even know why Vaughn wanted me to adapt my machine.'

'You say he intends to mass produce them?' mused the Doctor.

Watkins nodded wearily and hugged Isobel again.

The Brigadier was baffled. 'Why should Vaughn need such a weapon if he's already got the Cybermen?'

The Doctor suddenly perked up. 'Professor, you say you adapted your device to induce excessive emotional responses...?'

Watkins nodded and hung his head in shame.

The Doctor stood up and walked round and round the cluttered bench. 'Emotion is alien to Cyber neuro-systems,' he reflected. 'Perhaps it could be used to incapacitate or even destroy them... Yes, Vaughn obviously plans to use the machine against the Cybermen once he has no further use for them.' He gazed at his silent audience excitedly, then he hurried to the bench and picked up the circuits from the Hercules computer and from Jamie's radio. 'Of course. Emotional Induction.

How could I have been so stupid? No wonder the circuits aren't logical!'

Professor Watkins jumped up as if infused with new life and joined the Doctor at the bench. The two of them started muttering together and examining the circuits through magnifying glasses, totally oblivious of everyone else.

The Brigadier consulted his watch. 'Heavens, I must get back to the Hercules,' he exclaimed. 'I'm leaving at dawn for Geneva. Contact me at once if the Doctor comes up with anything, Jimmy,' he ordered and strode briskly out.

Zoe and Jamie glanced across at the bench. The Doctor and Watkins were deep in animated discussion over the oscilloscope. Jamie yawned cavernously and settled himself back in the armchair. 'Wake me if anything happens, Zoe,' he mumbled and closed his eyes.

Zoe gaped at him in disgust. 'You're incredible,' she exclaimed. 'You'd sleep through anything. For all we know, the Cybermen might be lurking beneath us at this very moment!'

Frantically Jamie struggled to shake himself free as the repulsive creature began to devour his foot. He woke with a start to find that Zoe was tugging his arm.

'Quick, Jamie, the Doctor's discovered something!' she cried.

On the wall the Doctor had sketched a large diagram showing the Earth ringed by a number of satellites and the Moon with the Cyber mother-craft on its hidden side. Professor Watkins, Isobel, Zoe, Jamie and Captain Turner gathered round as he explained his theory with mounting excitement. He drew a dotted line from the Cyber craft round the Moon to the side facing the Earth.

'Now, they'll move round and their transmitters will hunt for the frequencies used by these satellites,' the Doctor told them. 'The satellites will then boost their signals and relay them to Earth . . .'

'And the signals will activate these micromonolithic circuits,' put in the Professor, holding one up.

'Exactly,' resumed the Doctor. 'These circuits are

artificial nerve networks and once activated by the Cyber signals they will no doubt induce the hypnotic force being used to control the humans already in their power.' The Doctor held up the back of Jamie's radio. 'There must be hundreds of thousands of these circuits in International Electromatix components all over the world,' he concluded gravely.

'So everyone will come under their control,' Zoe murmured.

There was a shocked silence.

'Is there nothing we can do?' Turner asked earnestly.

Zoe clicked her fingers. 'The depolariser, Doctor!' she cried.

The Doctor beamed at her. 'Exactly, Zoe. What a good memory you've got.' He turned to the others. 'Fixed to the back of the neck, the depolariser can jam the control signals,' he explained.

'Neuristors!' cried Professor Watkins, turning to a large cardboard box filled with oddments. 'I think I've got a few here somewhere...'

'Splendid!' cried the Doctor, rubbing his hands together and springing to life again. 'Zoe, you help the Professor to make us some depolarisers. We'd better arm ourselves with immunity immediately.' He turned to the Captain. 'What time is it?' he demanded.

'Four in the morning, sir.'

'Please call the Brigadier on the radio. I'd better talk to him at once. The invasion could begin at any time!'

Within a few seconds the basement had been transformed into a hive of activity as the Doctor and his friends began the race to stop Vaughn and his alien allies from conquering the Earth.

The only sound in Vaughn's dimly-lit office was his calm rhythmic breathing as he lay tilted back in his chair, his lazy eye half open in macabre vigilance, the other peacefully shut. Suddenly a strident bleeping brought him instantly awake. He took up his fountain pen and twisted the cap. The wall obediently parted, exposing the wide-awake

Cyber Module whirring and prickling with intense light in the alcove.

'All is prepared?' it demanded.

'Of course,' answered Vaughn from the shadows.

'Invasion Zero will be one Earth hour from now. Countdown will commence now.'

'How melodramatic...' Vaughn smiled to himself as a regular electronic pulse started marking the seconds off one by one.

'We are moving into position to transmit the coercion signal. Transmission will commence in thirty minutes.'

'Yes, yes, yes, I'm well aware of the schedule,' Vaughn muttered sarcastically to himself, closing his eyes again.

Just then, Packer slipped noiselessly into the room from the private elevator. Vaughn swivelled in his chair. 'A few minutes, Packer... A few minutes and I shall control the entire planet,' he whispered, gazing out over the lights of the capital.

Packer glanced at the pulsing luminescent machine. 'You?' he murmured doubtfully. 'Are you sure of that?'

Vaughn's chair spun round to face him. 'Quite certain, Packer,' he snapped. 'Quite certain.'

The Doctor had done his best to explain to the Brigadier on the radiotelephone the exact procedure for constructing the vital depolariser jamming device.

'You must get them fitted immediately,' he repeated. 'If your technicians need any more advice just contact us here.'

'I'll get all my boffins on to it at once,' Lethbridge-Stewart assured him. 'Over and out.'

'Over and... and all that,' the Doctor muttered. He hurried back to the bench where Zoe and the Professor were hard at work making masses of fiddly connections. 'How many have you managed to knock together?' he inquried anxiously.

'Only five so far,' Zoe admitted. 'We can't find enough of those neuristor things.'

The Doctor looked worried. 'There must be some more

among all this junk . . . er, this equipment,' he said, starting to rummage frantically in the boxes littering the bench and piled underneath it. 'We've got to make enough for everyone here at least.'

Upstairs in the makeshift studio, Isobel had opened the blinds and was looking at the pale rose sky heralding the sunrise over the city.

'Penny for them,' whispered Jimmy Turner, appearing at her side.

She smiled wistfully. 'It's great. It all looks so peaceful.'

Turner agreed. 'Perhaps the Doctor's wrong about the invasion after all,' he suggested unconvincingly.

Isobel looked doubtful as she fingered the small cluster of transistors and wires taped to the back of her neck. 'He's been dead right so far,' she reminded him.

They watched a milkman making his deliveries to the houses opposite and a paperboy whistling as he cycled along the street. Then all at once they glanced uneasily at one another and Turner instinctively put his arm round Isobel's shoulder. The air seemed suddenly dry and brittle. A feeling of nausea swept over them and they felt a dull pain behind the eyes. A sudden crash outside made them look out again. Several milkbottles had shattered on the pavement and the roundsman was clutching his head and staring up into the sky. The paperboy took his hands off the handlebars and clapped them to his ears. Wobbling drunkenly, he careered across the street and crashed into the milk float. They heard a cry and heavy thump from the basement and then Zoe screamed.

They dashed out and down the steps under the stairs.

The Doctor was staggering round and round the basement in smaller and smaller circles with Jamie clinging to his arms in an attempt to prevent him injuring himself. At the bench, Professor Watkins was feverishly connecting some tiny wires with a soldering-iron.

Zoe glanced up as Isobel and the Captain rushed in. 'The

Doctor hasn't been fitted with his depolariser yet,' she cried anxiously.

The Doctor groaned with pain and collapsed in Jamie and the Captain's arms. They lowered him gently to the floor where he lay deathly still, staring sightlessly up at the ceiling.

'Hurry up, Professor . . . please hurry . . .' Zoe pleaded.

Watkins bustled over to them with the depolariser. They turned the Doctor over and Zoe carefully taped the lash-up to the back of his neck. Abruptly the Doctor went rigid with a spasmodic shudder.

'Doctor . . . Doctor, are you all right . . .?' Zoe cried, loosening his collar.

The Doctor lay prostrate, his breathing snatched and rapid and his eyes glazed over. They watched anxiously for some sign of revival. A tremendous crash from the street sent Isobel running back up to the studio.

A bus with a few writhing, goggle-eyed early morning passengers aboard had crashed into the milk float and steam was hissing from its ruptured radiator in a white jet. Then Isobel saw something that chilled her to the marrow. A heavy manhole cover in the middle of the street was suddenly flung into the air and it rolled clanging into the gutter. A gleaming silver figure clambered out of the sewer and stood with legs apart, swinging its masklike face to and fro in search of victims. It was followed by several more Cybermen and the group of malevolent giants strode off like figures in a nightmare, their blank eyes gaping and their slit mouths giving their faces a sinister, frozen smile as their thick, stubby fingers grabbed viciously at the air.

Isobel was transfixed for a few seconds by the awesome spectacle. Then she ran back down the steps into the basement.

The Doctor was sitting up and groggily massaging his temples.

'The Cybermen . . .' Isobel gasped. 'They're coming up out of the sewers . . . the invasion's begun!'

The Doctor blinked several times and then jumped to his feet, scattering his startled helpmates. 'Don't stand around like zombies!' he shouted. 'Don't you know the invasion's already begun?'

Zoe and Jamie tried to calm him, but he resolutely ignored them.

'Is everyone else all right?' he demanded, bustling round the basement as if nothing had happened to him. 'What about the Brigadier and the rest of UNIT?'

Captain Turner hurried to the radiotelephone. At last Lethbridge-Stewart came through faint and distorted.

'Chaos here, Jimmy. Only half the crew have recovered so far ...'

The Doctor grabbed the receiver. 'What about the other UNIT forces, Brigadier?'

'No hard news yet, Doctor. I'm sending Walters over there to pick you up. You'll be a lot safer here.'

The Doctor agreed. 'But be careful, Brigadier, the streets will soon be full of Cybermen.'

'Roger, Doctor. Just stay put,' the Brigadier ordered and clicked off.

Turner looked deeply disappointed. 'Sounds like a walkover for Vaughn and the Cybermen,' he muttered.

The Doctor nodded ruefully. 'And we're sitting right in the middle of the hornet's nest!' he sighed, trying to get rid of the irritating itch that was developing under the depolariser taped to his neck.

The sunrise flooded dramatically into Vaughn's office, lighting up his face with a dull red glow as he lay back in his chair listening to the incessant grating chatter of the Cyber Module.

'All areas are now covered by our transmissions. The full invasion force is mustering for despatch. Initiate ion beam for navigation.'

'All is ready,' Vaughn responded calmly.

'Prepare communication network for Cyberforce Control.'

Vaughn suddenly stood up. 'Wait. The Cyberforce must remain under my control,' he insisted.

The machine glowed brilliantly and the crystal whizzed back and forth agitatedly. 'Why do you oppose us?' it challenged him.

'I do not oppose you. We are allies,' replied Vaughn soothingly. 'But you do not understand the world as I do.'

The machine glowed even brighter. 'Humans are now under Cyber Control.'

Vaughn strode fearlessly across to the alcove. 'You will not achieve your objective unless I too get what I want,' he persisted. 'Is this agreed?'

The Cyber Module fell silent for a long time. Then it buzzed alarmingly and a smell of hot plastic filled the room. 'It is agreed,' it acknowledged eventually.

Vaughn smiled. 'Excellent. The invasion will proceed under my direction. Discussion terminated.' He twisted the pen cap sharply and the wall slid back into place.

As Vaughn subsided thankfully into his chair wiping the nervous sweat out of his eyes, the videophone bleeped and Packer appeared on the screen, his mean face pale and taut. 'Mr Vaughn, we've located the Professor . . .' he reported breathlessly.

'Excellent, Packer. Pick him up immediately,' Vaughn purred, hurriedly composing himself.

'But the UNIT mob, sir . . .'

'They will not offer any resistance. They are all under our control.'

'That's just what I'm afraid of,' muttered Packer inaudibly.

Vaughn leaned forward ominously. 'Packer, this is your last chance. Get Watkins and put him to work on the Cerebration machines at once,' he shouted.

After a terrifying drive through the chaos of disorientated humanity, Sergeant Walters skidded his jeep to a stop outside Professor Travers's house and ran up the steps. Captain Turner let him in just as the Doctor and the others came up the stairs from the basement.

'Thousands of them silver gnomes everywhere, sir,' Walters reported sturdily.

There was a scream of brakes outside. Turner slammed the door and shot the bolts home. 'It's Packer's mob,' he shouted over his shoulder. 'Out the back way quickly.'

As everybody turned and fled down the hall, a gun barrel crashed through the glass in the front door. Backing away, Turner fired his machine-pistol at the shadowy figures outside. The gun barrel fired a five second burst just as Jamie was ushering the Professor back down the cellar steps. The Professor cried out and staggered. Turner fired another burst then caught Watkins as he fell and slung him over his shoulder.

'Get out, Jamie!' he shouted, hauling the wounded Professor down into the cellar.

Jamie had paused to retrieve the radiotelephone unit which Turner had just dropped. As he started down the stairs after the others, another salvo from the front door caught him in the leg. He collapsed and started crawling to safety, dragging the radio behind him. The next moment, Sergeant Walters came running back up the stairs. He fired a long burst at the door and then carried Jamie out into the overgrown garden at the back of the house.

The others were waiting anxiously. Turner contacted the Brigadier on the Doctor's polyvox unit while Walters covered the rear of the house with his pistol. The girls tended the injured Professor and Jamie.

'We're in a bit of a spot, sir. Could you send us a chopper?' asked Turner.

'Wilco,' replied the Brigadier promptly. 'Can you reach Blue Sector Five?'

'We'll do our damnedest, sir, but we've got two wounded.'

'Right. Chopper on its way. Good luck, Jimmy. Out.'

Out in the street, Packer's jeep was speeding back to Vaughn's headquarters, leaving three security guards dead on Travers's doorstep.

Soon afterwards, Packer stood in silent humiliation in front of his master's desk.

'How?' Vaughn muttered, grinding his teeth in exasperation as he gazed out over the paralysed city. 'How can they be immune to the Cyber coercion signal . . . ?'

Packer shot him a crafty look. 'It must be that Doctor character's expertise. You should have eliminated him when you had the chance. Now he's out-manoeuvering you,' he whined accusingly.

Vaughn swung round from the window, his face a mask of contempt. 'I am still in control of the invasion, Packer,' he whispered hoarsely. 'Without me you would be wriggling like a worm in a puddle of acid.'

But Packer's defiance grew stronger and he faced Vaughn unflinchingly. 'We don't have the Professor, so we can't produce any more machines, so we can't control the Cybermen,' he rapped out harshly.

Vaughn stared at him with undisguised smouldering loathing.

'Do you still believe everything's going according to plan?' Packer went on recklessly. 'Do you still think you can win?'

'Contact the Antenna Unit. It is time to project the ion beam,' Vaughn suddenly snarled. 'The invasion force must be sent in at once!'

Packer's hand was resting on the handle of his pistol. He lingered for a moment as if undecided. Then he obediently picked up a telephone and rapped out an order.

The mighty Hercules whined reassuringly through the thin clouds. On the ground far below, all normal life had ceased within a matter of minutes as the millions of monolithic circuits scattered all over the world amplified and focussed the Cyber coercion beam being transmitted via the satellites from the neighbourhood of the Moon.

In the Operations Room, the Signals Officer was reporting the general situation. 'Washington's off the air, sir . . . Moscow and Peking dead as doornails . . . Nothing at all, sir.'

'Keep trying, Sergeant, all frequencies.' The Brigadier turned gravely to the Doctor. 'Seems to be a total radio blackout,' he murmured.

'Couldn't we make masses of these depolariser things

and distribute them to key personnel?' suggested Captain Turner.

The Doctor shook his head emphatically. 'No time, I'm afraid, even if we could obtain the components. The Cybermen will attack us in force soon. There must be an entire fleet out there, waiting behind the Moon.'

The Brigadier thumped his desk in frustration. 'We're utterly helpless...' he groaned.

'Unless we can stop the Cyber transmissions,' the Doctor mused quietly.

The Brigadier glanced hopefully at him. Then his face fell again. 'We'd need an orbital launch vehicle... We don't have anything of that size available.'

'Only the Americans and the Russians...' Turner sighed.

Suddenly the Brigadier stood up. 'Wait a sec!' he cried, going over to a security cabinet and dialling a sequence of combination codes. A drawer clicked open and he took out a thick file marked MOST SECRET and leafed quickly through it.

'I was right!' he announced delightedly. 'The Russians had a countdown in progress at dawn... unmanned orbital lunar survey. They must have a rocket almost ready to go.'

'So we could fit a warhead in place of their survey module,' Turner proposed brightly.

'Possibly, Jimmy.'

They turned to the Doctor inquiringly. He looked doubtful. 'How long would all that take?' he asked.

'We should be able to get a medical and technical unit there in a couple of hours, Doctor. Once we'd fitted the Russians with your depolariser things... well, it would be up to them,' replied the Brigadier. 'How long do you think we've got, Doctor?'

The Doctor shrugged. 'I confess I'm rather surprised they're not here already,' he said with a preoccupied air.

'Well, I think it's worth a try,' said the Brigadier, handing some papers from the file to Captain Turner. 'Here's the gen on the Russian launch, Jimmy. You deal with that top priority,' he ordered decisively. 'And get your skates on.'

Turner saluted and eagerly departed to prepare for his vital mission.

Just then the Hercules banked steeply and started to descend rapidly.

The Brigadier went over to the Doctor who was sitting withdrawn and thoughtful. 'Could we intercept the Cyber fleet with anti-missile missiles, Doctor?' he asked.

The Doctor cocked his head non-committally. 'Possibly. They'll be homing in on Vaughn's ion beacon out at the compound, I imagine.'

Lethbridge-Stewart consulted his Situation Map. 'Right. There's an RAF base at Henlow Flats equipped with Taktik missiles...' he muttered, striding down the busy Ops Room to brief his staff.

Zoe wandered in from up front and went over to the brooding Doctor. 'I think we're landing...' she murmured.

The Doctor stirred. 'Ah... how's Jamie's leg, my dear?'

'Just a flesh wound, but he's furious because the doctor won't let him walk on it. The Professor's okay too. Isobel's looking after him.'

'Jolly good,' muttered the Doctor vaguely. 'Zoe, I suggest you give the Brig a hand... much as I detest computers I suspect your remarkable little brain could be very useful to him in the next couple of hours.'

Zoe sniffed eagerly. 'All right, Doctor. What's cooking?'

The crumpled little figure seemed miles away. 'I think it's high time I had another little talk with Mr Vaughn...' he muttered absently.

Zoe gaped at him in disbelief. 'You're joking, of course,' she cried. 'Go back to Vaughn? He'll kill you as soon as look at you.'

The Doctor grinned bleakly. 'Quite possibly, Zoe, but we desperately need more time and I'm sure I can buy us that time.'

The Brigadier had overheard the little Time Lord's insane proposal. 'This is madness. I can't afford to allow you to try it,' he snapped.

The Doctor rose. 'You can't afford not to, Brigadier,' he retorted. 'Once you attack the Cybermen they'll retaliate.

We must know how and with what.'

Zoe looked sceptical and anxious for the Doctor's safety. 'How can you find that out?' she demanded.

With a mischievous twinkle in his eye the Doctor took out the polyvox unit. 'I'll leave this little toy switched on. You'll be able to hear everything that passes between me and Tobias Vaughn,' he explained.

The Brigadier snorted dismissively. 'But you'll never get near the place, Doctor. The city's crawling with Cybermen.'

'There's one place where there won't be any Cybermen now . . .' confided the Doctor, tapping his nose '. . . . In the sewers!'

At that moment the FASTEN SEAT BELTS sign lit up and a few minutes later the Hercules touched down on a remote disused airfield.

Zoe and Brigadier Lethbridge-Stewart stood at the bottom of the ramp waving goodbye and good luck as the Doctor drove the landrover out of the cargo bay. Tooting a jaunty farewell on the horn he sped off across the windswept grass-clogged concrete and disappeared.

'Take care, Doctor,' Zoe whispered, biting her lip.

Then a second jeep emerged down the ramp and stopped.

'The Tornadoes are due here in fifteen minutes,' the Brigadier informed Captain Turner. 'You should reach the Nykortny Space Centre in about two hours. Got enough depolarisers?'

'Yes, sir. The Professor's done us proud in spite of his wound.'

'Good luck, Jimmy.'

The jeep drove off towards some Nissen huts and the Brigadier led Zoe back up into the plane and the ramp closed behind them. In the Operations Room the Brigadier issued a string of curt orders right and left.

'Sergeant, ask Wing-Commander Robbins to take us to Henlow Flats Missile Base immediately and send a chopper to Blue Sector One in case the Doctor needs it. All

UNIT operational groups Red Alert Status.'

They were soon airborne again and it was not long before the Doctor's cheery voice came crackling over the polyvox receiver, echoing eerily.

'I've just entered the sewers and I'm making my way towards Vaughn's headquarters.'

'For God's sake, be careful, Doctor,' snapped the Brigadier.

'Oh, don't worry about me, the air's surprisingly fresh down here,' replied the Doctor earnestly. 'I'll call you when I reach Vaughn's. Down and out.'

'Over and out,' sighed the Brigadier anxiously.

'Your helicopter isn't going to be much good if the Doctor does meet any Cybermen down there,' Zoe remarked with a frown.

Lethbridge-Stewart flashed her an irritated glance. 'Perhaps I should send a submarine, miss,' he retorted defensively.

9
Counter Measures

Vaughn and Packer were poring over a vast map of the world. Outside the wide windows behind them everything was unnaturally quiet and still, except for the pigeons flapping over the rooftops and the odd car horn sounding under the slumped body of the driver.

'All main communication centres are now in the hands of our people,' Vaughn announced with smug satisfaction.

Packer looked unconvinced. 'But we can't do any more without the rest of the Cyber force,' he objected obstinately.

'They'll arrive, Packer, never fear. And when they do, there won't be a city in the entire world that we don't control,' Vaughn assured him in a strange singsong voice. 'Think of it, Packer... the entire world!'

A whooping alarm sounded from the video bank and the screens flickered automatically into life.

'Security alert,' Packer whined with a haunted look. 'The UNIT mob must have got through somehow.'

Vaughn glared at his Deputy and then punched a hold button as the screens flashed up a continuously changing sequence of views of the headquarters buildings. On one of the screens the Doctor's bulbous features loomed like a mischievous gargoyle.

'Good morning, Mr Vaughn, can you hear me?'

'Yes,' Vaughn hissed into the desk microphone, his eyes burning with hatred.

The gargoyle grinned. 'Oh, jolly good. Hope I haven't dropped in... or rather popped up at an awkward moment, but I'd rather like a word with you,' the Doctor said breezily, straightening his rumpled collar and brushing his lapels.

Vaughn smiled acidly at the microphone. 'Clever of you to outwit the coercion beam, Doctor.'

The Doctor shrugged modestly. 'Well, to tell you the truth it's been a bit of a pain in the neck,' he quipped cheekily. 'Shall I come up? I do know the way.'

The mocking face vanished from the screen.

'He must be out of his mind,' Packer exploded.

'Far from it, Packer. Make a security check in case he's brought any friends with him again,' Vaughn ordered calmly.

Packer spoke tersely into his wrist radio.

'We'll kill the bastard this time,' Packer resolved, his beady eyes glinting.

Vaughn sighed with infinite patience. 'No, Packer, we will do no such thing. You forget the Doctor's travel machine. He's our insurance.'

The whine of the Hercules's turboprops faded as the UNIT Airborne Operations Unit touched down at Henlow Flats Missile Base north-east of London.

'Stand by, raiding party. Defensive stance. Attack only if necessary,' snapped the Brigadier, buckling on his pistol.

At that moment, the Doctor's voice came through again on the polyvox receiver. 'Just about to enter the lion's den,' he reported. 'I'll leave this thing switched on now . . .'

The Brigadier wished him luck. Then he ordered the Signals Desk to keep the channel open. 'Get the whole lot on tape. If he needs help throw in everything we've got in Blue Sector.'

Zoe hurried in carrying a box of depolarisers which she and the Professor had managed to cobble together. 'Hope there'll be enough to go round,' she said.

The Brigadier complimented her warmly.

They froze as a cultured voice purred silkily from the polyvox speaker. 'Ah . . . Doctor . . . What an unexpected pleasure . . . Come in and sit down . . .'

Zoe wanted to stay and listen, but the Brigadier took her firmly by the arm. 'Come along, Miss Zoe, and keep close to me. We've got work to do,' he ordered.

Seated in a comfortable chair, the Doctor had listened to Vaughan's arrogant story with inward contempt but with a smile of respectful admiration playing on his mild features. As his host fell silent, the Doctor studied him with thinly veiled incredulity.

'And you trust these Cybermen?' he exclaimed.

'I know them' Vaughn boasted, dramatically silhouetted against the panoramic windows. 'I know the way they think... their single-minded purpose...'

'Then you must realise that they are ruthless inhuman destroyers.'

'Naturally, Doctor. I have worked with them for five years on this project. They are my allies, not my enemies,' Vaughn purred.

The Doctor raised his dark eyebrows. 'You actually believe they'll honour the bargain you have made with them?'

Vaughn squinted imperiously down at the small, hunched figure sitting opposite. 'I planned this whole operation, Doctor,' he claimed with smouldering passion. 'It was I who contacted them far out in the Solar System. They are merely providing their strength and technological skill to fulfil my vision.'

The Doctor leaned forward, his eyes like gimlets as they searched into Vaughn's. 'In return for what? What do the Cybermen gain from it all?' he demanded.

Vaughn chuckled throatily. 'What they want and what they get are two very different things, Doctor.'

The Doctor was not impressed. 'Two can play at that game. Once the invasion is completed they'll just toss you aside like a spent cartridge.'

Vaughn leaned forward in turn. 'All Cybermen are programmed to obey my orders, Doctor,' he smirked.

'Oh, your bunch of silver sewage workers might be. But what about the ones sitting out there around the Moon?'

challenged the Doctor. 'Will they do as they're told, Vaughn?'

Vaughn hesitated. For the first time his eyes betrayed a shifty uncertainty. There was a tense pause. 'If they do not, I shall destroy them with the Professor's machine,' Vaughn retorted.

The Doctor snorted. 'With one single solitary device?'

'More will be made.'

'Not without the Professor's help. And we have the Professor.'

Again Vaughn hesitated, deeply troubled but still smiling smugly. 'I have no reason to doubt my allies,' he murmured.

The Doctor stood up. 'You can't possibly take such a gamble!' he cried earnestly. 'If the Cybermen do take control of the Earth, they will destroy all life as we know it.'

Vaughn walked round the desk, smiling malevolently. 'You're just playing for time,' he sneered. 'You presumably managed to protect your UNIT cronies from the coercion signals. What exactly are they up to now?'

'You are living in a fantasy world,' the Doctor shrugged calmly.

Vaughn flicked a switch on the desk. Packer appeared on a monitor screen. 'Are the ion beam transmitters aligned?' he demanded.

'Affirmative. The fault's just been rectified,' Packer replied.

Vaughn switched Packer off and took out his fountain pen.

'Your friends are too late, whatever they're trying to do,' he crowed triumphantly, twisting the pen top.

The astonished Doctor watched in horrified fascination as the wall opened to reveal the Cyber Module spitting and sparking in its lair.

'Your delays must cease forthwith,' rasped the machine. 'Transporters are prepared to launch.'

'We are locking on now,' Vaughn confirmed.

'Confirmation Invasion Fleet First Stage completed,' the machine croaked. 'Second Stage initiating now . . .'

The Doctor shielded his eyes as he tried to study the sinister alien apparatus from the other side of the office. 'This is madness, Vaughn. You must stop now!' he burst out, gazing momentarily at the brilliant, flashing crystal and covering his seared eyes again.

But Tobias Vaughn was trembling with fanatical determination. 'You don't understand . . .' he whispered. 'I can't see all those years of work wasted. I must go on!'

In the small concrete control block set within a massive bunker buried in the middle of the Henlow Flats Missile Base, teleprinters clicked quietly and radar sweeps silently tracked round and round and back and forth. A dozen Air Force personnel lay slumped over the computer guidance and radar terminals, apparently dead. At the Controller's desk mounted on a raised central dais, a young Squadron Leader was hanging over the arm of his revolving chair, a red telephone receiver still tightly gripped in his nerveless hand.

Suddenly the door flew open. Lethbridge-Stewart quickly appraised the situation and strode in followed by Zoe and four troopers.

'Get these chaps fitted up with depolarisers,' he ordered, after checking one or two pulses.

While Zoe and the troopers set about taping the neuristor assemblies to the backs of the airmen's necks, the Brigadier called the Operations Room on his polyvox unit.

'What's the state of play, Walters?'

'Captain Turner reports that he's just crossed the Russian border, sir.'

'What about the Doctor?'

'So far, so good. We're getting it all on tape, sir.'

The Squadron Leader moaned and stirred into consciousness.

'Excellent, Sergeant. Stand by . . .'

The Squadron Leader stared up at the hazy figure and blinked dizzily. 'I'm . . . I'm Bradwell, sir . . .' he stammered, trying to get to his feet and collapsing back into the chair. '... Were we attacked...?' he mumbled, attempting a salute.

The Brigadier waved away formality. 'Just you relax and try to clear your head, Squadron Leader,' he ordered gently. 'Then I'll fill you in.'

Twenty minutes later most of the bunker personnel had revived and Bradwell was gazing incredulously at the Brigadier.

'But it's utterly fantastic...' he gasped as Lethbridge-Stewart finished the hurried briefing.

'But true I'm afraid, Bradwell. We're expecting the invasion fleet at any moment. If they get here intact we've all had it.'

The Squadron Leader stumbled groggily over to the radar screens. 'See anything, Peters?'

'Not a glimmer so far, sir,' responded the Flight Lieutenant manning the main scanner, rubbing his temples tenderly.

'We could be too late,' murmured the Brigadier.

Zoe joined them. 'What's the maximum radar range?' she asked.

'Pretty accurate to about ten thousand miles, miss. Dodgy outside that,' Peters replied.

'Then we won't see them until they're almost on top of us,' she sighed downheartedly.

'All the same, we can certainly arrange a little reception committee for them,' Bradwell muttered, turning briskly to his team. 'Begin fuel priming and countdown prelims...' he ordered.

While the pre-launch procedures were smoothly completed, the Brigadier called the Ops Room on the polyvox again.

'Has Turner reached Nykortny Base yet?' he demanded impatiently.

'No word yet, sir.' Walters smartly replied.

'Something now!' shouted Flight Lieutenant Peters. 'Just on range limit, sir. Faint but closing very fast.'

The Brigadier rushed over to the radar display. 'This it?'

he asked curtly.

'Looks like it, sir...' said Bradwell, pointing out a dim group of white dots near the edge of the main screen.

Peters keyed in a command and a complex of symbols was superimposed on the display. 'They're on a ballistic trajectory, sir... in range approximately five minutes from now.'

'Where are we on prelims?' snapped Bradwell.

'T minus forty five seconds, sir,' called a voice from the launching section.

'*Hold*!' rapped Bradwell.

There was a rapid succession of shouts and acknowledgements.

'Holding at T minus forty-five, sir.'

'Prepare fuse locks and run arming code...' Bradwell ordered, going to his desk on the dais.

Zoe peered at the radar. 'Look! There are more of the things now.'

'Arming codes running . . .'

'There's hundreds of them now!' shouted Peters.

Squadron Leader Bradwell turned to the Brigadier. 'We can't possibly take out all of them, sir.'

Lethbridge-Stewart nodded stoically. 'Just get as many as you can...' he said quietly.

Behind Bradwell the computer discs and spools whirred busily.

'Link programme to telemetry guidance,' he commanded.

Zoe had been carefully studying the host of invasion craft on the screen. 'I think you could knock out a good ninety percent of these things,' she announced unexpectedly.

'Nowhere near enough Taktiks,' snapped Bradwell, absorbed in his checking schedule.

Zoe bridled at his dismissive manner. 'It's no use just blowing up half a dozen or so,' she persisted. 'Those things are in tight formation patterns. If you guide each missile carefully I'm sure you could set up a chain reaction.'

Bradwell considered for a moment and then shook his

head. 'There isn't time to compute all the variables, miss. The things will be on us any minute now.'

Zoe grabbed the Brigadier by the arm. 'I know I can do it. Just give me thirty seconds,' she begged.

Bradwell looked at her as if she were mad. He glanced at the Brigadier who looked unhappy and undecided.

Then Lethbridge-Stewart remembered the Doctor's words about the girl's extraordinary capabilities with computers. 'All right,' he sighed. 'Give her thirty seconds.'

Flight Lieutenant Peters swung round in alarm. 'Sir, doesn't give us much time to . . .'

'Revised countdown to begin at T minus forty five in thirty seconds from . . . *now*!' Bradwell interrupted.

Zoe was already at the Guidance Programme VDU, calling up data and scribbling feverishly on a notepad. Bradwell tapped his fingers impatiently on his console and the Brigadier fiddled anxiously with the polyvox unit while they waited for the outcome of Zoe's calculations. At last she ripped a sheet off the pad and thrust it at Bradwell.

'Enter this into the guidance programme!' she urged him confidently.

Bradwell glanced at the list of numbers Zoe had scribbled and then handed it to the Guidance Programmer. 'You'd better be right, miss . . .' he frowned, as the man began furiously typing at the keyboard.

'T minus forty five seconds from . . . *Now*!' Bradwell ordered, returning to his console.

Once again the systems buzzed into life and the discs and tapes spun madly back and forth. The Squadron Leader inserted a key into his console. 'T minus thirty seconds . . . No hold-ups now, please,' he prayed, his eyes flicking over the check panels. 'T minus ten . . .' He turned the key decisively.

'Data accepted, sir!' someone reported.

Zoe folded her arms and crossed her fingers. The Brigadier stared at the vast invasion fleet spread across the radar scanners.

'Three . . . two . . . one . . . Fire!' Bradwell pressed a button.

Out on the airfield, the small compact missiles streaked

out of their silos in groups of ten and vanished immediately into the haze.

Inside the bunker, everyone crowded round the radar screens and held their breath. There was a long, agonising pause while teleprinters chattered out ballistic data and guidance details, but all eyes were on the multitude of white blobs on the radar.

Suddenly, one by one, and then in gradually increasing numbers, the blobs began to vanish from the screens as the Cyber fleet was blown to smithereens just above the Earth's atmosphere . . .

The Doctor had been keeping as quiet and unobtrusive as possible while he watched the titanic struggle of wills between Vaughn and the Cyber Module.

'You have betrayed us, Vaughn,' shrieked the machine. 'The Transporter Fleet has been attacked and virtually destroyed.'

'That is not possible,' Vaughn protested vehemently. 'You are trying to blackmail me.'

'You have failed, Vaughn. We shall take control now.'

Desperately Vaughn sought for some delaying tactic. 'Give me time. I can deal with the saboteurs,' he pleaded.

The Module sparked angily. 'There is no more time.'

Vaughn's eyes betrayed his bluff. 'I will not allow the invasion to proceed unless I control it,' he boasted.

The machine paused as if listening, its crystal bristling with millions of brilliant pinpoints of light. 'We no longer require your services, Vaughn,' it screeched. 'We shall dispatch a Megatron Bomb. We shall destroy every living thing . . .'

The Doctor went ashen. 'A Megatron Bomb!' he gasped. 'So this is your great vision, Vaughn . . . to be master of a dead world.'

All remnants of Vaughan's confident and complacent charm finally dissolved under the Doctor's scornful gaze. In an instant he shrank into a spiteful, whining dwarf. 'You can't destroy the world,' he screamed at the Cyber Module. 'What about me?'

The Module crackled menacingly. 'You are superfluous, Vaughn. The invasion will succeed. The bomb will be dispatched forthwith.'

Vaughan laughed manically. 'You'll destroy your own Cybermen here.'

'The sacrifice will be small,' rasped the machine.

Vaughn kicked the desk like a petulant child. 'I won't allow it!' he shrieked, red-faced and trembling.

'You cannot stop us, Vaughn.'

The Doctor went over to the almost hysterical figure. 'Now perhaps you'll believe the truth. You cannot make bargains with Cybermen,' he muttered grimly.

Vaughn shoved him aside. Seizing the Cerebration Machine from the desk he advanced on the alcove. 'You think you're indestructible...' he sneered. 'But I can destroy you... all of you.' He touched some switches and trained the projection horn of the device directly at the glittering crystal.

The Professor's machine emitted its clicking and then its piercing whistling noise and the Cyber Module immediately began to vibrate and strobe crazily.

'Opposition is futile...' it croaked, as smoke began to belch from its melting connections. Trickles of liquified metal ran in rivulets down the vacuum tubes and they started imploding, with sharp glass splinters flying everywhere.

Vaughn gloated over the disintegrating apparatus like some insane magician. Boosting the output of the quivering device in his hands, he laughed in a crazed, hollow voice.

The Doctor did his best to wrest the machine out of his grasp, but Vaughn simply nudged him aside, yelling at the top of his voice: 'I'll destroy them all... I'll destroy them all...'

'Turn it off, man!' the Doctor shouted. 'You're going to blow us all sky high.'

Suddenly there was a gigantic ripping sound and the crystal broke into millions of tiny fragments. Vaughn and the Doctor were hurled back against the desk and the Doctor managed to wrench the Cerebration Machine away from Vaughn and turn it off. A flurry of smaller explosions burst out like firecrackers, scattering debris all over the office.

When the smoke finally cleared, all that remained of the Cyber Module was a shapeless mess of twisted silicon and glass and a tangle of swollen and slit-open wires smouldering poisonously in the gloom.

Zoe was lifted shoulder-high and cheered by the enthusiastic bunker personnel.

'Knocked every single one for six!' exclaimed Squadron Leader Bradwell. 'Quite fantastic. How did you do it, miss?'

Zoe shrugged coolly. 'All quite logical really. Just a question of speed, mass, angle of descent, angular density... Stuff like that,' she smiled.

'Can we keep her, sir? She's much prettier than a computer,' Bradwell laughed.

The Brigadier shook Zoe's hand. 'Well done. Jolly good show,' he said with a sombre smile.

All at once Benton's distorted voice buzzed from the polyvox in the Brigadier's pocket.

Lethbridge-Stewart whipped it out. 'What's the flap?' he demanded.

'We overheard something on the polyvox from Vaughn's place, sir... Apparently the Cyberforce is going to fire some sort of bomb at the Earth. It's called a Megatron or something. Could wipe us all out...'

The Brigadier cast his eyes wearily up to the ceiling. 'So all our efforts here mean nothing...' he muttered through clenched teeth.

A dismal silence fell over the blockhouse.

The Brigadier rallied himself with an attempt at morale boosting. 'Where there's a will...' he muttered. 'Right, Benton, tell the Wing Commander to prepare for take-off. We're coming back over at once. Out.'

'We'll keep in touch on this open line,' he told Bradwell, handing him the polyvox unit, 'then you'll know what's going on. You might try and get a fix on that bomb...' he added doubtfully.

Bradwell grinned. 'Don't worry, Brigadier. If we do, we'll try and set it off on its way in!'

With a nod of thanks to the bunker crew, the Brigadier led Zoe and his UNIT squad back to the Hercules out on the runway.

Gradually Vaughn's manic laughter died away and he leaned on the desk muttering agitatedly. 'It's dead, Doctor... It's dead... I killed it...'

'But you haven't destroyed the Cyberforce,' the Doctor earnestly reminded him. 'They are still out there, preparing to obliterate your planet.'

'Five years work, Doctor, and all gone in less than five seconds.'

The Doctor seized Vaughn by the shoulders and shook him vigorously. 'Listen to me,' he persisted. 'You must switch off the ion beam. No doubt the Cyberforce will try to use it to trigger the Megatron Bomb!'

Vaughn stared blankly back at him, his mouth forming inaudible words.

'We are both allies now,' the Doctor argued forcefully. 'Both fighting for our lives. You must stop the beam.'

Hazily Vaughn focussed on the Doctor's wildly persuasive eyes. 'The ion beam... yes... Packer must switch...' He moved slowly round the desk like a sleepwalker and touched a button.

The monitor screens lit up. On several of them loomed the stark silver images of Cybermen.

'Packer... Packer... where are you...?' Vaughn cried in a strangled voice into the microphone.

At that moment the door slid aside and Packer burst into the office. 'Vaughn... what have you done?' he screamed. 'They... the Cybermen have taken over... They won't obey... They've killed several...' he whipped round gaping in terror at the open door. 'They're coming after us...'

Then Packer took in the devastation still smouldering in the alcove. He flew at Vaughn screaming uncontrollably: 'What have you done to us...?'

Before Vaughn could react, a Cyberman appeared in the doorway. Packer snatched out his pistol and emptied the magazine into the monster's rasping chest grille. Then Vaughn dived behind the desk and the Doctor seized the Cerebration Machine and scampered into the smoking alcove. The Cyberman's laser unit emitted a series of blinding flashes and Packer's body seemed to alternate from positive to negative in the blistering discharge. His uniform erupted into flames and his exposed skin crinkled and fused like melted toffee papers.

From the alcove, the Doctor aimed the projection horn and switched to full power, shutting his eyes and mentally muffling his ears against the intolerable whistling from Watkins's sinister apparatus. The Cyberman took a few lurching strides towards him and then slowly folded over like a broken doll with viscous smoke spurting from its joints and shrill metallic screams from its slit mouth.

With a grunt of congratulation to the absent Professor for the efficiency of his device, the Doctor switched it off and put in on the desk. Then he pulled the trembling Vaughn to his feet.

'Where is the ion beam control?' he demanded.

'We can't fight them...' Vaughn whimpered, gazing down at Packer's hideously incinerated body.

'Where? Where do we switch off the beam?' the Doctor repeated, shaking Vaughn.

'At the compound. But they'll be there too...' Vaughn murmured.

The Doctor took out the polyvox unit. 'Brigadier, can you hear me?'

'Affirmative, Doctor. We heard everything. What do you want us to do?' rapped Lethbridge-Stewart.

'There are two possibilities,' the Doctor hurriedly explained. 'Either we switch off the ion beam or we destroy the Cyber Mother Craft...'

'Well, Doctor, Captain Turner reports that the Russians are cooperating magnificently, but it'll take at least ten hours for their rocket to reach the Cyber ship.'

The Doctor drummed his fingers anxiously along the

casing of the polyvox unit as if it were a penny whistle. 'But their bomb could be sent at any moment, Brigadier. The ion beam's our only hope.'

He turned to Vaughn. 'Will you help us to cut off the beam?' he pleaded. 'We'll never do it in time unless you help us.'

Vaughn gazed at him cynically. 'Why should I help you?'

'To save the world, Vaughn.'

Vaughn laughed. 'And if I survive, Doctor... What future have I? What will the world do with me now?' he scoffed wearily.

The Doctor glared fiercely up at him. 'For goodness sake, stop thinking about yourself,' he shouted. 'Think of all those millions out there...'

Vaughn regained a trace of his old bland composure. 'Appealing to my better nature, Doctor?' he smiled. Then his face hardened. 'No. If I help you it will be because I hate the Cybermen.' He turned and gazed out over the sunlit city. 'I know you think I'm insane, that I want power for its own sake. But you're wrong. The world is weak, a chaos of conflicting ideals. It needs a strong, single-minded leader. I was to be that leader...' His voice broke with emotion.

'Vaughn!' the Doctor begged him.

Vaughn turned round. 'I'll help you,' he agreed in a dead voice. 'But only because they destroyed my vision, my dream.'

Vaughn walked like an automaton over to the Cerebration Machine, stepping unseeingly over Packer's corpse. 'We must get to the compound at once,' he said mechanically.

The Brigadier's voice buzzed out again. 'Doctor, we have a chopper in the area. Can you get onto the roof?'

'Yes, Brigadier. We're on our way now. Up and away...'

'Out, Doctor.'

Vaughn picked up the Professor's device. 'Your UNIT friends are most efficient, Doctor, but we shall need this. The Cybermen will be guarding the ion transmitter.'

Eyeing the apparatus warily, the Doctor cautiously followed his unexpected ally to the elevator.

10

The Nick of Time

As the Hercules lumbered into the sky and turned slowly north-east, the Brigadier marshalled his scanty forces for a desperate last stand against the Cyberforce and their Armageddon device – the Megatron Bomb.

'Where are we off to now?' marvelled Isobel, joining Zoe in the Operations Room.

'Reinforcing the Doctor. He's going to fight his way through a couple of hundred Cybermen.'

'Golly,' cried Isobel, her eyes shining with admiration.

'I've only got a platoon,' Lethbridge-Stewart reminded them. 'No time to find more neuristors and revive more of my men.'

Just then Captain Turner came through on the radio. 'The Russians have just launched their rocket,' he reported faintly from the Nykortny Base. 'Supercooled Hydrogen Warhead. Should do the trick, sir.'

'If it gets there in time,' murmured the Brigadier pessimistically. Keep me posted, Jimmy.' The Brigadier shook his head and laughed drily. 'An American warhead stuck onto a Russian missile . . . There's hope for the world if only we can save it now . . .' he mused.

Immediately afterwards, the Doctor was heard on the polyvox unit shouting above the roar of the helicopter which had picked him and Vaughn off the roof of the International Electromatix Headquarters.

'Brigadier! We're about to land in the compound. We must go straight in, I'm afraid.'

'That's madness, Doctor. We're right behind you. Wait

for us.'

'Don't worry, Brig, we've got Watkins's machine,' retorted the Doctor. 'It's proved most effective against Cybermen so far.'

Lethbridge-Stewart realised it was useless to object. 'If you insist, Doctor.'

'Vaughn says the ion beam is transmitted from the blockhouse under the three spherical antennae shrouds.'

'They look like three giant golf balls,' added Zoe helpfully.

'Roger, Doctor.'

'Down and out,' cried the Doctor as the helicopter began its descent.

'Infuriating man!' muttered the Brigadier to himself, glaring at the polyvox unit.

The cockpit intercom clicked on. 'Ten minutes to touchdown in Red Sector One,' announced the Wing Commander.

The Brigadier turned to Corporal Benton. 'Alert assault platoon for immediate disembarkation!' he snapped.

Zoe and Isobel edged forward. 'Can we come with you?' asked Zoe.

'Please. It'll be my last chance to photograph Cybermen,' Isobel added. 'Golly, what a scoop!'

The Brigadier shook his head resolutely. Then he looked them up and down. 'I don't know about a scoop . . .' he muttered, relenting. 'But I suppose the archives in Geneva will be glad of . . .' He paused and grinned. 'Just keep out of my way, that's all.'

Vaughn clasped the Cerebration Mentor to his chest as he and the Doctor ran through the maze of buildings forming the factory complex, making their way towards the distant blockhouse under the three spherical antennae shrouds. They had successfully dodged patrolling Cybermen, but suddenly one of them appeared abruptly round a corner, striding inexorably towards them. Vaughn stopped and carefully aimed the apparatus at it. At once the Doctor grabbed his arm and dragged him into a doorway out of sight.

'What do you think you're doing?' Vaughn muttered distrustfully. 'We must destroy them . . .'

The Doctor peered warily round the corner. 'They don't know we're here yet. Let's keep the element of surprise.' He looked again. 'All clear now.'

Reluctantly Vaughn agreed and they crept along the side of the enormous building and started to run down a narrow alleyway. Just ahead of them a door opened and they were confronted by two silver giants completely blocking their escape. Vaughn aimed and triggered the machine. A shrill whistling bored into their heads and the two Cybermen performed a hideously comic semaphore of jerking limbs, with smoke and black fluid-like pus oozing from their joints and grilles.

'Now they'll know we're here,' lamented the Doctor as they clambered over the hot, smoking carcasses and rushed on down the alley.

Reaching the end, Vaughn indicated the roofs of a group of derelict buildings opposite. 'We can go up that way . . .' he panted, racing across a yard to a rusted fire escape.

The corroded structure creaked and wobbled as they stumbled round and round the spiral staircase and onto the roof twenty metres above the concrete. Dodging between the shattered skylights, rusted ventilator cowls and sagging beams, they made for the other end of the vast ruin. Vaughn paused to look over the edge and then opened a steel door in the head of a shaft.

The Doctor peered into the unwelcoming darkness. 'Is this the only way?' he asked unenthusiastically.

'It is now,' Vaughn told him. 'The Cybermen are all around us already.'

Before following Vaughn down into the gloom, the Doctor scanned the sky hopefully. But there was no sign of the Brigadier's forces. He glanced over the parapet. Cybermen were striding across the small yard and along the alleyways far below. With a brave shrug he started down the echoing concrete steps.

The UNIT taskforce screeched to a halt in the compound and leaped from their jeeps.

'There are the golf ball things,' shouted the Brigadier, 'over that way through the old buildings . . .'

Zoe and Isobel ran along behind him. Isobel was laden with camera, lenses and rolls of film.

They made their way through a deserted old factory building and were about to cross the yard beyond it when the Brigadier ordered the force to take cover behind the inert and decaying machinery.

Silhouetted against the sunlit open doorway stood four Cybermen, their huge shadows stretching across the floor. The UNIT platoon concentrated its machine-gun fire on the advancing enemy, but it had no effect whatsoever. Then the Cybermen's laser units flashed with intense blue light and two troopers were flung against the corrugated steel wall of the factory amid splinters of wooden crate.

'Bazookas! Where the hell are you?' yelled the Brigadier, glancing over his shoulder at two groups of soldiers frantically setting up a pair of anti-tank launchers behind a massive lathe.

'Fire at will!' he ordered, grabbing Isobel as she tried to take a telephoto shot of their assailants and dragging her back beside Zoe behind a huge steel pipe.

All at once there was a roar and a searing whoosh as the bazookas fired. The Cybermen were hurled cartwheeling and disintegrating out of the building by two devastating explosions.

'Advance!' ordered Lethbridge-Stewart, leading the way.

Isobel could not resist stopping for a moment to photograph the tangled remnants of the Cybermen. 'Great!' she murmured, her motorised shutter zipping madly away.

'Come on!' Zoe urged her. 'That's only four of the monsters.'

They followed the troopers across the yard and into the alleyway opposite.

Vaughn and the Doctor froze momentarily as the sound of muffled explosions rumbled through the semi-darkness inside the old powerhouse.

'That'll be the Brig,' the Doctor murmured with satisfaction as he followed Vaughn among the eerie ghosts of the heavy machinery.

Eventually Vaughn forced open a small door and they emerged into a narrow road running alongside the windowless blockhouse containing the ion beam generator. Vaughn pointed up at the flat roof under the three shrouded antennae.

'That's the best way into the building,' he advised. 'Take them by surprise.'

The Doctor glanced cautiously round the edge of the door. 'It's very odd, Vaughn. There don't seem to be any Cybermen here at all.'

Vaughn indicated the corpses of several security guards lying near the entrance to the blockhouse. 'No doubt they are all inside, Doctor,' he murmured. 'I'll go up there first and cover you.'

The Doctor waited while Vaughn clambered up the fire escape at the corner of the transmitter building. When he reached the top, the Doctor edged out into the road and scuttled across to the foot of the stairs. As he reached the corner, three Cybermen suddenly emerged from the open door of the powerhouse where he had been crouching seconds earlier.

'Behind you, Vaughn!' he yelled, dodging round the corner out of sight under the metal stairs.

Above him, Vaughn spun round aiming the Professor's machine awkwardly over the handrail. As the intense whistling ripped the air, one of the Cybermen collapsed in a heap of wobbling limbs and tubes. Before Vaughn could adjust the direction of the horn, the other two Cybermen discharged their laser units simultaneously. Vaughn was instantly transformed into a pillar of fire, flickering rapidly from positive to negative. He flung the Cerebration Machine high into the air and it smashed asunder at the Doctor's feet in a cascade of delicate components. Vaughn's terrible death took several seconds as he flailed about in a vortex of strobing white flames.

Crouching beneath the fire escape, the Doctor's blood ran cold as he listened to Vaughn's final agonised screams... They were the sounds not of a human but of a Cyberman. When he looked up eventually, the Doctor felt a rain of fine black ash on his face.

Rubbing his watering eyes, the Doctor peered round the corner. The second Cyberman had now collapsed on top of the first, but the third monster was advancing across the road towards him. Glancing behind him, the Doctor saw that the alley formed a dead end. The hissing rubbery breaths were only metres away. Swallowing hard, the Doctor waited at the corner. As soon as the creature appeared, he dived forward between its legs and raced towards the powerhouse door.

At the far end of the road, the Brigadier and his troops saw the disorientated Cyberman trying to disentangle itself from the railing of the fire escape. Behind it, a tiny figure scurried into the powerhouse.

'There's the Doctor!' cried Zoe.

'Bazookas!' snapped Lethbridge-Stewart.

Seconds later a roar burst from the launcher and the Cyberman was blown to pieces in the middle of the roadway.

After a pause the Doctor crept out from the doorway. 'Where on earth have you been?' he yelled. Then he pointed to the blockhouse. 'The ion beam transmitter's in there... Do get a move on...'

Led by the Brigadier, the platoon and the girls tore down the road to the blockhouse. After a brief consultation with the Doctor, the Brigadier ran up the fire escape, clambered over Vaughn's welded corpse and onto the roof. Armed with her camera, Isobel tried to follow him, but the Doctor caught her and dragged her under the fire escape. Several troopers clattered after the Brigadier and the others surrounded the blockhouse with levelled machine-guns.

After a long silence they heard a tinkle of glass followed by several grenade explosions. The door of the blockhouse was blown off and a number of Cybermen staggered out to be greeted by a hail of machine-gun fire.

Isobel wriggled out of the Doctor's grasp and took a series of hurried pictures of the heap of wriggling, gasping aliens scattered over the roadway. More massive explosions followed and more Cybermen tottered into the dense barrage of bullets and collapsed twitching and smouldering on top of the others.

There was a long silence. At last the Brigadier staggered out, coughing and wiping his blackened face to hearty cheers from his men. He found the Doctor posing heroically on the fire escape, flourishing bits of dismembered Cyberman while Isobel snapped cheerfully away.

'When you're quite ready, Doctor...' he gasped resentfully, 'we have an invasion on our hands.'

The Doctor grinned cheekily at him. 'Oh really, Brig? It looks like soot to me!'

In the Henlow Flats bunker, Squadron Leader Bradwell and his team listened to the Brigadier's Situation Bulletin on the polyvox unit while keeping their eyes fixed on the radar scanners for any sign of the Cyber Mother Ship or of the Megatron Bomb.

'... By destroying the ion beam transmitter we have stopped the enemy triggering their bomb. However, their Cybership continues to transmit its hypnotic signal and therefore the world remains paralysed,' explained Lethbridge-Stewart. 'To stop this signal we must eliminate the Cybership. The Russian rocket should reach it in... in approximately six hours. If the warhead succeeds then humanity will be released from Cyber coercion and we shall be able to mobilise International Defences against the Cybermen already on the Earth...'

'Something on the screen, sir!' called out Flight Lieutenant Peters. 'It's coming in very fast.'

Bradwell hurried over. On the edge of the long-range sky radar was a large white blob. 'Sure it's not noise, Peters?'

'No, sir, it's there all right. True orbital path. Must be gigantic.'

Bradwell snatched up the polyvox. 'It must be the Cyber craft,' he murmured.

'It's in a holding orbit, sir. Approximately five thousand miles.'

The Squadron Leader apologised for interrupting the Brigadier. 'We've picked up an enormous UFO, sir. It's orbiting about five thousand miles out.'

'Outside your range I suppose?' asked the Brigadier despondently.

'Oh yes, sir. Anyway we've only got some odds and ends left. We chucked all our best stuff at the earlier lot.'

Lethbridge-Stewart grunted. 'Very well. Thank you, Bradwell. Inform me of any change. Out.'

In the Operations Room inside the Hercules the atmosphere was fraught with anxiety. The Brigadier told Benton to contact Captain Turner at the Nykortny Base in Russia. Then he turned to the Doctor, who was silently brooding by himself.

'Why the devil would they move their Mother Ship in to a closer orbit?' he asked, completely mystified.

The Doctor roused himself. 'No doubt to deliver their bomb,' he mused.

'But Doctor, we've destroyed the ion beam transmitter . . . so how . . . ?'

The Doctor sighed. 'I must have been mistaken,' he confessed. 'Evidently the device does not require an ion field. However, if as I suspect it is highly unstable, then it must be confined within a giant magnetic field until shortly before detonation. Therefore it could hardly be fired by missile from the neighbourhood of the Moon some 230,000 miles away . . .'

'You mean the magnetic field has to be generated inside the Mother Ship?' Zoe blurted out.

The Doctor nodded gloomily. 'Precisely, Zoe. So they have come in closer to Earth and are presumably about to launch the Megatron Bomb.'

'So they must have come in range of the Russian missile!' exclaimed Zoe excitedly.

'Indeed, Zoe, but unfortunately travelling in the wrong direction.'

The Brigadier put up his hand for silence as Captain Turner's voice at last came through. 'Sorry about the delay, sir, but we've had an almighty flap on here...'

'Can the Russians re-direct their rocket, Jimmy?' demanded the Brigadier urgently, his eyes fixed on the Doctor's.

'Yes, they already have, sir. Estimate contact with Cyber craft in fifteen minutes.'

The Brigadier glanced at his watch. 'Could the Cybermen deliver their bomb in that time?' he asked the Doctor.

The Doctor nodded, gripping Zoe's hand protectively. 'Easily, I'm afraid.'

The Brigadier thanked Turner and sank into a chair. 'This is going to be a long fifteen minutes...' he sighed.

They sat in agonised silence, waiting. Once Benton knocked a tin mug flying and it clattered under the radio console, making everyone jump. The hapless Corporal mumbled his apologies sheepishly.

After a seemingly eternal vigil Squadron Leader Bradwell's excited voice burst from the polyvox receiver. 'We have the Russian rocket on radar, heading right on target, sir.'

Then a chorus of urgent voices was heard in the background. 'Now we've got a third echo sir, heading *away* from the Cyber ship!' Bradwell shouted above the hubbub in the bunker.

The Doctor stood up, frantically ruffling his mop of hair as he glanced at Zoe in despair. 'The Megatron Bomb...' he whispered. 'It's on its way after all...'

In the bunker at Henlow Flats Squadron Leader Bradwell stared at the three traces on the radar screen. The small trace of the Russian rocket was fast approaching the large blob of the Cyber Mother Craft. A third echo, the Megatron Bomb, was moving rapidly away from the Mother Ship and towards the centre of the screen.

'Prime all remaining Taktiks,' he suddenly rapped out. 'Override checks programme and link into skyprobe radar guidance.'

'Target trajectory linked...' reported Peters. 'In range thirty seconds. You think this will work, sir?'

'No idea, but we've got nothing to lose,' Bradwell cried cheerfully, the light of battle shining in his eyes. 'Guidance locked on yet?'

'Best we can, sir, on all three missiles.'

Bradwell turned the key in his command console. 'Right. One at a time... Three... two... one... Fire!' He stabbed the launch button with crossed fingers.

The bunker crew waited tensely.

'One's going wide, sir...' Peters called out.

'Prepare Two and standby Three, just in case.'

On the other side of the airfield the two remaining missiles had swung their slim black noses up at the sky. Seconds later one of them streaked away into the blue.

'Two looks good, sir,' Peters reported.

On the radar scanner the Taktik missile was soon seen homing in directly on the Megatron Bomb missile, while far beyond them the Russian rocket was now almost touching the Cyber Mother Ship.

'Bradwell, what the devil's going on over there?' the Brigadier suddenly boomed from the polyvox unit.

At that moment a frenzied cheer erupted in the bunker.

'Bradwell...? This is Lethbridge-Stewart. I demand to know what's happening...'

Another even bigger cheer and whoops of delight filled the bunker as the airmen hugged one another and shook hands.

Bradwell picked up the polyvox. 'Two bullseyes, sir!' he reported, laughing with relief as he gazed at the tracer sweeping back and forth across the blank radar screen.

'Not a trace of 'em left.'

While the Brigadier's and the Doctor's hearty congratulations buzzed out of the polyvox unit, Bradwell reached under his collar and gingerly removed the depolariser taped to his neck. It had begun to itch...

Two days later, Zoe was once again posing under the hot lights in Isobel's improvised studio. This time she was wearing a black catsuit and her hair was covered in silver glitter, while Isobel looked cool and relaxed in orange hotpants and silver boots.

'What exactly is this new job you've landed?' Zoe asked, taking a well deserved breather.

'It's super,' Isobel grinned. 'Because of all my action photos of the Cybermen I've got an exclusive contract with a magazine to do a worldwide exclusive on the invasion! What about you, Zoe?'

Zoe screwed up her face. 'Oh, I suppose when the Doctor's finished repairing the TARDIS circuits we'll be off again,' she replied regretfully.

Isobel looked sad. 'Where to?'

Zoe shrugged. 'We never know where to... or *when* to, come to that,' she replied mysteriously.

The door burst open and Captain Turner popped in.

'Here's my dolly soldier at last,' cried Isobel.

'Cheeky!' grinned Turner. 'Zoe, the Doctor's ready to leave. I've got the jeep outside.'

Zoe looked a little downcast. 'Oh, any news of Jamie?' she asked.

'He's fine, Zoe. We'll pick him up from the hospital on the way.'

Isobel nudged Turner mischievously. 'Could I come too?'

Turner hesitated. 'Okay, as long as you promise not to call me your "dolly soldier" in front of the Brig,' he warned her sternly.

They all laughed and he led the way outside.

An hour later, the Doctor, Zoe, Jamie, Isobel, Captain Turner and the Brigadier all climbed out of a UNIT jeep parked beside a gate leading into a field.

'Here, Doctor?' exclaimed Lethbridge-Stewart, surveying the leisurely cows with some misgiving.

'Yes, thank you, Brigadier, this is fine,' smiled the Doctor, opening the gate. He turned and shook hands warmly.

Jamie limped up and frowned. 'Och, are ye sure this is the place, Doctor?'

The Doctor shielded his eyes with the two repaired circuit panels and surveyed the placid rural scene. 'Yes, Jamie. Don't you recognise that cow over there?'

They followed his arm and gaped in astonishment. Half the cow seemed to be missing - only its head and forelegs were visible.

The Doctor chuckled. 'The TARDIS must be just over there. Come on you two, all aboard.'

He marched across the lush grass and went up to the half-invisible cow. He patted its head tenderly and then took a few steps towards where its tail should have been and promptly disappeared. Immediately his head reappeared just above the cow's head.

'I've found the TARDIS!' he cried. 'Hang on a minute while I put the circuits back.' Again the Doctor disappeared.

'What the devil's the fellow up to?' muttered the Brigadier scratching his head, while Zoe and Jamie exchanged a grin.

A few minutes later, the TARDIS materialised with fitful flashes of its yellow beacon and shrill grindings from its innermost mechanism.

'A disappearing police box!' gasped Isobel, opening her camera case. 'I don't believe this . . .'

The door opened and the Doctor emerged. 'Come along, you two!' he shouted. 'We're five hundred years late already.'

Zoe and Jamie bade farewell to the amazed and bewildered group at the gate and walked off arm in arm towards the shabby police box. Isobel clicked eagerly away as the intrepid trio stood waving in the doorway of the TARDIS, with the Doctor posing dramatically for the telephoto lens. At last the door squeaked shut.

Isobel, Captain Turner and the Brigadier leaned on the gate and laughed as the cows suddenly looked up and scattered in all directions mooing loudly. With a hoarse trumpeting and groaning sound the battered police box faded and finally vanished completely.

'Where do you think they've gone, sir?' asked Turner, shaking his head in puzzled disbelief.

The Brigadier watched the cows as they gradually resumed their quiet grazing. Then he shrugged. 'It's a moot point, Jimmy,' he said and marched briskly back to the jeep.